CATHY COOTE

INNOCENTS

GROVE PRESS
New York

First published in Australia in 1999 by Random House Australia Pty Ltd.

Published simultaneously in Canada
Printed in the United States of America

FIRST AMERICAN EDITION

Library of Congress Cataloging-in-Publication Data

Coote, Cathy, 1977–
    Innocents / Cathy Coote.
        p. cm.
    ISBN 0-8021-3927-2
    1. Teacher-student relationships—Fiction. 2. Teenage girls—Fiction. 3. Seduction—Fiction. 4. Australia—Fiction. I. Title.

PR9619.4.C66 I66 2002
823'.914—dc21   2002021465

Grove Press
841 Broadway
New York, NY 10003

02 03 04 05   10 9 8 7 6 5 4 3 2 1

M

y darling,

All of this is my fault.

I know you think you're to blame for what happened. You're wrong, my love. I've been guilty all along.

I hardly know where to start.

Start at the very beginning.

The very beginning seems so long ago, though. I'm hardly interested in it.

I suppose, at the very beginning, you must have seen my legs.

That isn't fair. I'm not for one second suggesting that my legs were what you were after.

There were legs *everywhere*. It *was* a girls' school. It *was* PE day. There were hundreds of us. We were, all of us, in netball skirts. They were horrible, scanty, red-pleated things, obviously designed by a pervert. They showed your bum when you bent over, so you had to wear little shorts underneath. The little shorts were called 'scungies'. They were off-red, and looked the way the name sounded. We also had semi-transparent

V-necked white shirts. Red trim pointed like an arrow at our bellies. I had a red hair-ribbon in my hair.

I was, as always, amazed at my ability to blend in with the masses of us. I kept assuming that eventually, inevitably, I'd be standing in a crowded place and suddenly everyone would start shifting uncomfortably and turning their heads at the smell of *other*. A ring of empty space would start to form around me as the people shrank away, and I'd be left standing on my own, irrefutably alien.

I dreaded that moment. My whole life was geared around avoiding it.

The recess before I met you passed like any other.

I met my friends for lunch behind the library.

I sat cross-legged on the grass, nibbling at my thin vegemite sandwiches. Before me, a row of girls perched on the rickety wooden bench. Those few stragglers—like me—who arrived too late to get a spot on the bench had to sit on the ground.

I would have preferred to sit in the shade. I hated to feel the sun on my skin. I was frightened of that pitiless, slow sense of burning, the creeping pinkness on the back of my neck. I never said so, of course.

Rachel always sat in the hottest spot she could find. ''S good for my tan.'

Tans were important. Tanned skin was *normal*.

The others made fun of Gothic Anita, the witch of Year Ten, with her talcum-powdered face.

'Looks like a witch!'

'Looks like Dracula! Stupid cow.'

So I squared my shoulders, and sat as I always did with the

rest of the group. I laughed along with them, through my nose, contemptuously, abandoning my skin to the full light of the sun. It seemed like a small price to pay.

My skin meant very little to me, in those days.

'Fuck, she's a loser!' said Rachel in disgust.

'I reckon,' agreed Sally, opening her Mars bar.

King and Queen condemning a leper, they nodded towards Anita, who stood down by the fence that marked the boundary of the oval, sharing a surreptitious cigarette with a passing civilian.

We all agreed that yes, Anita was a loser.

Sally went on, 'Look at that *crusty* she's with!'

Anita's friend on the outside sported a nose-ring, and wore a grubby poncho.

'She's *foul*.' I agreed, my voice one of six or seven chorusing confirmation.

I knew it was wrong to condemn a fellow freak like this. But I didn't feel guilty. I had to protect myself.

'D'you know what she did at camp? Last year?' Rachel asked Sally. Her question was interactive. It was meant to be overheard.

'Oh—' Eyebrows communicated silently. '... d'you mean ... with Kelly?'

Rachel nodded significantly.

'What?' asked Laura, sitting on the grass next to me.

There was a conspiratorial silence.

'*What*? What did they do?'

'They're *lesbians*,' revealed Kara, leaning in eagerly from the end of the bench.

Slightly ruffled at this usurpation, Sally asked, 'But d'you know what she *did*?'

My sandwich finished, I chewed my nails. I had a vague flash of a daydream, in which some power grew in me, so that I was able to dismiss their nastiness with polished indifference: able to turn my eyes blue like icy lasers on them, cutting through their babble with one diamond-edged remark.

Instead, I found myself sniggering along, slightly louder than the rest, to call attention to my surrender and maximise its worth.

'Yeah,' said Kara. 'She got into Kelly's bunk and started to *finger* her, and Kelly didn't *mind*. She *liked* it!'

'Yu-u-uck!' I said, over three syllables.

'That's *gross*!'

'I *know*,' Rachel said, popping a stick of chewing gum into her mouth. Rachel never ate at recess. She said everyone knew you put on more weight in the morning.

'And Mrs Lamonde finds them and she goes, "What are youse doing?" and Anita goes, "Kelly's scared of the dark."' Kara really knew her stuff.

Anita, in the middle distance, threw her cigarette over the fence onto the path. She and her visitor laughed.

'Fuckwits!' said Rachel, examining her cuticles.

I nodded.

(This isn't much like your one-in-six-billion girl, is it, darling? *You* thought I was perfectly, instinctively original.

Once, in the car, you pulled over just to tell me, 'I never know what you're going to say *next*!' You were so excited! You stroked my cheek with your thumb, speechless with love and admiration.

You've no idea, have you?—how much I'd have given, just to be able to slide down into the barely conscious state in which the flocks of schoolgirls existed. They were like a swarm of bees. They all changed direction at the faintest whiff of pheromone. I'm convinced that most of them had no individual consciousness at all. When you're genuinely enthusiastic about netball, you don't need a sense of yourself as a distinct entity. A sort of share in the group consciousness, like a cable extension, is quite enough for all the thinking you ever need to do.)

We sat in an acrid, disapproving semicircle, all arms folded.

'She's foul!'

'I reckon!'

'She's got a pet *rat*!'

'That's gross!'

'It lives in her *room*!'

'Probably sleeps in her *bed*!'

'She's a *freak*!' declared Sally.

She was quite right. Anita *was* a freak. She made herself into a freak. She wouldn't have been like us if you'd paid her. She marked herself a freak carefully, thoroughly. She wore a size eighteen uniform on a size fourteen body. Her dumpy form always looked *wrong* in the school tartan, even after the teachers had confiscated her bracelets and rows of earrings, and made her tie her mottled, bottle-black hair back in a neat ponytail. Her unstitched hemline always wavered far below her knees, trailing threads. Splotches of red paint from an Art class clustered over one hip. 'She's had her rags today!' ran the joke, every, every, *every* day, long after the stains had faded to a distinctly non-menstrual pink colour.

'What's she doing *now*?' Rachel asked, with weary disgust.

Elbows straight, Anita gripped the top of the fence, bending forwards. Her head and torso were outside school property. Her boots scrabbled for purchase in the wire mesh below.

'Her legs are fat,' complained Amy.

'Is she fucken ... leaving?'

'She is!'

'Dob her in!'

'Yeah, tell on her!'

But she wasn't leaving; she was breathing. Her face thrust close to her friend's, she hissed a guttural '*Haaaaaaah!*'

The crusty woman shook her head, still laughing, and waved her hand before her nose.

'Her breath prob'ly *stinks*,' decided Rachel, with easy hypocrisy. She smoked Marlboros behind the bus shelter every morning before school, instead of having breakfast.

'Smells like Kelly's underwear!' suggested Kara, giggling.

Laura squealed: 'Oh, you're foul!'

'That's *disgusting*,' ruled Sally.

'I *know*!' I said.

Then the bell went, and we straggled up the hill for English.

Walking through the corridors, I followed the loud voices and the laughter of the others. I was one little fish in an enormous shoal, changing direction effortlessly at the slightest twitch of the leader's tail. I blended in perfectly, as usual. No-one suspected a thing.

I can't remember if I even knew we were getting a new teacher. Everyone said Mrs Bohringer had run off with Mr Russell who was head of Maths and they'd both been fired. I'd heard that Lucy Hinds' sister Kerry had seen them kissing in the supplies room. It was a scandal. I giggled along with it. But I don't think I seriously believed it was true.

Anyway, I wasn't expecting to see you standing, hands clasped gently in front of you, behind the teacher's desk.

In we all trooped and sat down.

INNOCENTS

You had chalked your name on the board in huge white letters. I think you stammered slightly when you introduced yourself. You wore a tweed suit that was too big for you, in the most expensive and well-tailored way imaginable. I've always liked your taste in clothes, darling. There's a faint sort of mad-professor quality that goes with your bedraggled hair. I don't think you mean to look like that; it's just an accident of your wardrobe and distraction. I suppose that's what's so charming.

I didn't pay you the slightest attention.

I just sat at my desk, up the back by the window, reading a book, through the whole lesson. You didn't tell me to stop. I assumed you hadn't seen me.

The book was *If This Is a Man*, by Primo Levi.

I know you've read it, though we've never discussed it. It's on the bookshelf in the study. It's hardcover and some of the passages are underlined in passionate biro, presumably by you. I'm sure it's the sort of book you'd love, come to think of it. I'm sure it's one of your special ones.

It's about the Holocaust. It's about concentration camps and the fetid depths of man's inhumanity to man. I often used to read books like that.

I read them because I needed to confront myself, head-on, with what I was. Poor Primo, trapped without hope of escape in the very lowest circle of hell, keeps popping up with remembered scraps of poetry and resolutions to shave every day, no matter what, to preserve his human dignity. As you read, of course, you're completely on his side, cursing the Germans, cursing their cruelty. You can't understand where it comes from, all that violence, that will to subjugate.

You droned on, my darling, about iambic pentameter. You made a few well-worn jokes. You called Shakespeare *Bill*.

No-one laughed. My friends slumped, chins on elbows, lethargic hands scribbling away on pencil cases.

Did you see something in my face, even then? Did your eyes, skimming across that legion of indifferent faces, stop for a second and linger on mine?

I find it difficult to believe. In those days, I counted myself lucky to look so uninteresting.

When I considered my looks, which was rarely, I thought myself distressingly bland. Eyes just seemed to slide off my face. All my features were too even to excite the vision. In the bathroom, in the mornings, before I'd wiped all the sleep from my eyes, my face was a ghastly white blur which fizzled out in the ill-defined, pastel-yellow halo of my hair. My straining eyes could not even see themselves.

My body was small and neat, which was good for my purposes. A spy needs firstly to avoid looking like a spy. A successful traitor, even more than a loyal subject, must appear to conform. I was saved from obesity, crustiness, overtallness. I was therefore saved the accusing, conspiratorial glares that were thrown about regarding Anita, that girl with the infant dreadlocks, the broad shoulders, the nose-ring that teachers continually growled at her to take out.

As we all filed out at the end of class, you stood beside the door.

'Good book?' you asked me as I passed.

I can't remember what I answered. I think I ignored you.

I lived with my aunt and uncle in a drab brown house that backed onto the road reserve.

They were decent people. Decent enough, anyway, to take

me in and care for me from the age of four, paying my school fees and driving me to endless games of netball. They were also decent enough not to have had any other children to rival me when the chocolate biscuits were being distributed.

My uncle was a thin man, with a thin moustache and thinning hair. He came from Queensland. He dressed like a Queensland primary-school headmaster. Striped short-sleeved shirt and ill-matching tie. Shorts—the formal sort, belted. Socks pulled *right* up and folded over just below the knees.

He never said much over dinner. He watched cricket. He smelt of stale sweat on Saturdays when he came in from mowing our lacklustre, sunbleached lawn.

He was a nice man. He gave me pocket money if I asked for it, and picked me up at 10 p.m. from school discos, asking dryly, 'Did you pull?'

I always said, 'No!' as though the idea disgusted me, and he always replied, 'Next time, love,' as though he were commiserating me.

My aunt was flabby and pathetic, with a turkey-chin and small sunken eyes. She draped her big body in floral fatlady dresses. She babbled insincere bitchings about the women she worked with. She ate and ate and ate. I often found chocolate wrappers in the bathtub. She was like a large passionless sponge.

I won't say I never saw my aunt in tears, or that no emotion at all was ever expressed in that household. It's just that it all came at inappropriate moments.

She could say, 'Your Mummy's gone to Heaven' (stupid, banal phrase!—it makes my blood boil to think of her using it), 'You'll be coming to live with us now,' but her tone was as workaday as the lino that covered our kitchen floor. Her *delivery* was all wrong.

On the other hand, one afternoon when my uncle came home from the shops with the wrong sort of biscuits—caramel Tim-Tams instead of normal ones—I saw the tears come coursing down her cheeks. I thought they'd never stop. Her dimpled chin shook and wobbled as earthquakes of emotion passed through her.

'It's such a *simple thing*!' she wept, her big face flushed a passionate red.

I stood in the kitchen doorway—I must have been about twelve—and watched her grieve like the Mother of Christ after the Crucifixion, her heavy head bowed down over the biscuits, her hands over her eyes.

My uncle, trying to apologise—and to hide his frustration at the embarrassing tides of emotion pouring out of his wife— also proved himself to have more than just the one bland, everyday face.

'I'm sorry,' he said, silhouetted against the bright white window. He reached out a hand and laid it, in a futile gesture of comfort, on my aunt's heaving shoulder. He held himself like a Hollywood actor at a moment of high crisis, speaking in short, significant sentences. 'I'm really sorry.'

It would be comforting to think that some of the blame for my perversity could be unloaded onto my aunt and uncle.

It is true that there was always a feeling in that house ... not of active resentment, so much as of being slightly put-upon, of having an extra chore to perform, one more thing to do, one more bill to pay. There were a lot of short sharp sighs, especially from my aunt.

Even the most saintly child—if she was sensitive and intelligent—would have found it difficult to be happy in that household. The unhappiness, for me, all centres on small details: my uncle's pockmarked cheeks, his trouser-shorts, the faded orange-and-yellow linoleum on the kitchen floor. My aunt's big, cheap floral frocks drying inexorably on the clothesline.

But for anyone with any powers of reason to deny their own responsibility for their situation is just silly. For all I know, my own parents may have exuded just that air of workaday stodginess, and I'd still be what I am.

This remembering is so strange! It's like trying to think back over last night's dreams at five in the afternoon.

When I think of those days, I think of myself bobbing up and down in an ocean of mundanity, all soaked and sozzled with it. I think of my fat aunt hunched over a carton of ice-cream at the kitchen table. Such a commonplace, everyday gluttony. Such an understandable craving.

It will be hard to look at the pages ahead. I will cover each completed line as I write, so that I don't have to look back on them. Even scrawled in this exercise book, for no-one's eyes but yours, they will parade my shame.

First of all, darling, I have to make it clear that *I am not what I was*. I am no longer afflicted by the visions I'm about to describe.

I have you to thank for this. I owe you all my gratitude, and yet, naturally, I'm very reluctant to explain exactly why. How can I show you the hideous, clinical calculations whirring away beneath those lips that brushed your cheeks so lightly it made them itchy, whispered ticklishly in your ear, 'Oh, I love you so much it's giving me a *stomach ache*!' and made you blush?

My love, you have exorcised fouler demons from me than you can possibly imagine.

I'm tiptoeing around this subject, aren't I? Teasing you with fleeting references, whispered insinuations. Just the way I used to powder your face with filmy kisses, arousing you with the excruciating airiness of my touch.

Here, then. Feel the terrible solidity of the truth.

I drew my own pornography—carefully, carefully, it was my life's work—and stored it in the bottom drawer of my desk.

What a filthy, skulking creature I was! I coasted along through the corridors of the school, stealing images and transmuting them. With my mind, I peered under blouses and up skirts. I peeled away the uniforms to poke at what was underneath.

My perverse gallery, at the time that I met you, filled three sketchbooks and two-thirds of a fourth.

In retrospect, I suppose the pictures were not pornography, but something worse. Pornography suggests a desire to ogle, to leer, but all the same, it is only looking. My gallery was a gallery of depraved erotica, of props in a vicious saga. The black-and-white sketches were palmcards in my technicolour inner monologue.

I constantly told myself instalments of the same story. The drawings were stills of the most climactic moments. Scene by scene, I humiliated, commanded, penetrated. I laid my classmates on their backs and I spread their legs and sent hard cold objects into their most secret recesses. I oversaw their torture.

I whipped them, kicked them, spat into their faces.

The central theme of each scene was the same: *I was in control.*

I don't mean I was some ridiculous Madam Lash character saying 'Lick my boots.'

I didn't appear, as such, at all. I wasn't there in person, exactly, with my physical characteristics. It was more like watching a person-eye-view movie. I was an abstract controlling force, giving orders as if from behind an opaque screen.

An important thing I've just realised is that I was never, ever, *ever* involved sexually, myself. It was all about the sexual humiliation of the victims. But it had nothing to do with my physical arousal.

I didn't masturbate.

Or rather, my masturbatory activities were centred on the biggest and most responsive organ of all the erogenous zones— my mind. I'd lie on my bed, my chin resting on my folded hands. The sketchbooks would be flung wantonly before me, open at select images. I'd look, and look, and look, becoming drunk on physical details, until I could close my eyes and see the figures moving—coloured now, living, breathing, animated—in a perverse home movie.

Oh how can I begin to show you the contours of my perversion? Your exploration destroyed these lands, darling. Your touch tore them like cobwebs. They dissolved fizzing under your spittle.

I still have maps.

The geography is precise and vast. Closing my eyes I find myself outside the gates of my old primary school, St Luke's. The courtyard led into the Science labs at St Mary's, the school where I met you. Out one door there was the school gym. Through another door lay an oval, any oval. Past the oval, trees. Past the trees, a swimming pool. Cartoon blue water, sunk in concrete and confined by a high wire fence. I know every inch of this.

By the light, it is late afternoon. They are nearby, always. By the twisting in my stomach, they are just now being formed. I'll stroll my bodyless presence out onto the oval and see who's being made.

What kind of mind is this? It gives me golems to use as lovers. Here they come, in answer to my impatient summons. They're sulky but obedient. Obedient to my sulky will.

This nervous creature my soul presses up against my eyelids, leering.

I'm violently thrilled. It seems like a licentious oversight, a cosmic loophole, even in this spectral land, that I'm allowed to. That no-one can stop me from—

I yoke a golem. She's all body. I don't see her eyes. I see breasts, cunt, wrists and ankles. Sometimes a mouth.

Open, I cry.

I need to, I cry.

I'm going to, I cry.

And there is nothing she can do.

And that's why.

Appendages to my estate sometimes came and went. I remember that, after we went to the beach one year for Christmas, months of my stories were set in a huge, rambling towerblock filled with empty, self-contained apartments like the one we stayed in.

It is to my shame that the continued suffering, the ongoing subjugation of my victims, was necessary to my scenarios. The bits of stories I have written down are examples only. In reality I continued them from day to day, like a soap opera.

Of course, there were certain taboos.

No blood, including menstrual blood. The skin was never broken. No permanent injury. Nothing which might scar or break a limb.

None of my victims was ever cut when I whipped them. Bruises, on the other hand, were permissible. They did not bleed from the vagina when I raped them. Sometimes there was the nebulous idea of administering a kind of drug which would force them to orgasm against their wills. In this way, an act which, psychologically, constituted a rape, betrayed none of the physiological signs of one.

There was no death. I instinctively loathe the idea of sex-murders, of cannibalism, dismemberment, autoerotic asphyxi-ation. I feel the same bewilderment and disgust when I read about madmen who kill prostitutes or rentboys, keeping the bodies in pieces in fridges. I feel no camaraderie with such men.

These thoughts that swam like fish through the oceans of my consciousness flap disgustingly about, here on paper. I'm frightened that, instead of looming hugely dark and terrible, as they seem to me, they will be laughable. I'm worried that I'll find myself in the same category as the skulking middle-aged men who open their trenchcoats to schoolgirls in train stations. The girls are meant to scream in terror before the sinister power of the erection, but invariably they shriek with laughter, hissing hysterically to one another: '*Gross!*'

*

I was addicted.

I couldn't sleep if I didn't.

Afterwards, in the silence of the sleeping house, my scalding mind a little cooler, it might be possible to read a book or listen to a CD. But before—no chance.

There were nights that I tried to restrain myself. Every week brought a new resolution, a moment of stoicism, when I raised myself through sheer determination, up out of the power of my corrupt and dangerous mind.

I would stay downstairs watching television, talking nothings with my aunt, cooking, folding the laundry, until I was sent to bed. Dragging my feet, I'd trudge up the stairs, and spend far longer in the bathroom than was necessary.

Once in my room, I'd turn on the radio for company. Searching my mind for innocuous images, I'd make pencil sketches of landscapes, or fish, or trees. If I could set myself an absorbing enough task, I'd manage to maintain a fierce interest in it until two or three in the morning. Then I'd sink into bed, exhausted, and let sleep claim me.

This never worked for more than one night.

By morning, I'd be tense as a cat. If my aunt or uncle spoke to me at breakfast, I wanted to spit at them over the cornflakes. If, in the crowded corridors of the school, anyone brushed me as they passed, I'd jolt with the shock of it.

My skin crackled with electric sparks. My chest grew tighter and tighter all day. My fingernails would start to dig painfully into my palms. Some small humiliation—an inability to answer a question in class, or a passing sarcasm from Rachel—'Nice hair'—would set me off.

A cold fury would build, aided and abetted by an acute awareness of the sensuousness of my surroundings: in the classroom, the polished wood of the chairs; outside, the wind against my cheek; everywhere, the very motion of my body against the air as I walked.

The simple act of breathing became charged with an unbearable eroticism.

All afternoon my stomach would twist and turn with anticipation. I tried not to leer—*I tried not to be seen to leer*—at the short tartan hemlines of the thronging child-women around me. My eyes took in the forms of the girls, smooth legs slim waists small breasts, and set them to dancing in my mind.

Walking home along the road reserve, I had no eyes for the swaying trees on the pathside prairies around me. I was shivering on some level beneath my skin, with a kind of premonition of what was to come.

As soon as I got home, I'd race up the stairs to my bedroom and lock myself in.

I paced my room, striding five steps across, or four from the door to the desk, in an agony of restlessness. I turned the music up too loud, trying to make it shout my frustrations for me.

I burned with bleary hatreds.

I swore and swore at the girls in my class. I assembled them in front of me, and for once they were silent; they could not reply.

I spat at the parade of thighs arses bellies breasts, and hid my head under the blanket. But the darkness only seemed to encourage my macabre menagerie. They came dancing on relentlessly, flaunting themselves, begging me to step in, announce my presence, take control.

There was no other way into oblivion. There was no other way to buy peace.

*

Not quite the 'earthbound, perplexed angel' you describe in the journal you left behind, am I?

Yes, darling, I knew about your little shrine to me, stashed in a desk-drawer.

In that tabernacle I recognised three of my essays, a ruler I thought I'd lost, and a page of abstract sketches and doodled phrases another teacher once confiscated from me. There was also a copy of a class photograph from the year before, where I sat with the other short girls in the front row, my hands folded in my lap.

In that austere, black and red hardcover notebook, you gave vent to your earliest passions, scrawling formless longings, bits of thoughts, speculations. It's the patchwork that results from a dizzying obsession.

How I can ever have managed to appear 'like a stray angel, whining divinely at the door' to you, I can't imagine. I think of myself as having been furtive, catlike, selfishly cunning.

'Always gazing, entranced, at nobler dimensions than this one' is more plausible. Burdened with my secret, I went through the motions of life distracted. At school, I was often in trouble for not taking enough notice in class. Seized with a sudden paroxysm, I would scribble obscure notes to myself, or make uninterpretable diagrams, whatever the situation. My other teachers were not impressed.

You're convinced I was 'dainty'. I know I was just small.

There are also photocopies of a kind of official case-history in this drawer. I suppose it was on file at St Mary's. It details my orphaned status. On the back, you've written: 'a dispossessed darling, all silent and alone … whatever does she think all day?'

Reading that wakes a dreadful retching feeling in my stomach.

I'm thinking now of a different drawerful of oddments, connected with a different obsession. It was in the bottom left drawer of the pine desk that stood against the window of my bedroom, back in my aunt and uncle's house. That was where I used to keep my little stash of pictures.

I've done a sketch like the ones that used to fill those books in my bottom drawer. I have to shock myself into an understanding of what I was. It's too easy to gloss things over with words. I've tacked it up on the wall, a foot from my face.

I still can't believe it's anything to do with me.

The pencil sketch shows a girl. Her long hair hangs over her face as she bends her head, looking down. She is without clothes or background props—her body floats in the white space of the page.

She has—I can't believe that the phrases exist in my language, in any language, to write such a thing impassively!—she has a one finger up her vagina. The rest of her fingers are splayed out over her crotch. With her other hand, she holds a breast.

It doesn't excite me, although the figure came easily to my mind and I drew without hesitation. There are echoes of arousal—my heart quickens imperceptibly, my eyes linger—but it is a *remembered* desire, like the phantom passion of an impotent man.

Forgive me, forgive me, forgive me.

I know you're not a voyeur, darling. You're too kind a man to be titillated by something that's brought me so much misery.

I know that, even now, you're probably shaking your head, muttering, 'You don't have to tell me all this.'

Please bear with me. I have to confess *everything*.

Darling, I was a better person then. At least in those days nothing impinged on the world. I went about, bubbling and boiling, but I was bordered off, a kingdom in myself. That degeneracy seems strict and noble, compared with what I became.

I was effortlessly amphibious, strolling calmly about the surface world of school playgrounds, shopping trips with my aunt, school discos ... and then, once I was alone, plunging into the submerged depths of my psyche.

I can honestly say that I had no idea about the turmoil bubbling away behind your wistful jokes and concern about my essays. I didn't really notice you, at first, what with my distracted state of mind.

Your interest in my schoolwork was like so much background noise.

Lots of teachers knew I was clever. My aunt, if she hasn't thrown them out, has shoeboxes full of my old report cards, all saying how much potential I had, if only I would apply myself; or how intelligent I obviously was, except for my irritating tendency to daydream in class.

It's strange, to think that, while I was worrying about another realm of existence, just steering myself through our conversations in the same way I negotiated playground politics, you were busy falling in love with a phantom.

In the first few weeks, you were just another of the obstacles I had to navigate every day. Once, you called me back after class to discuss an essay.

As we all came strutting past, you singled me out, beckoning casually. I stopped by your desk. You were looking straight at my midriff. You toyed with a pencil, trying to seem bored, duty-bound. I turned my gaze out the window, the one that showed into the corridor, and looked at the reflections of empty desks. You must have been acutely conscious of the way I leaned forward, resting my stomach on the worn wood of the desk. It wasn't deliberate, though.

The last stragglers went out the door and turned down the corridor, their voices dying swiftly away.

'Right,' you said, professionally. You pulled out your prop —my essay—from under a sheaf of papers.

'Right,' I said. I came and stood behind you, and to one side, leaning over, regarding the essay. I was thinking about leather bindings and the delicate wrists of schoolgirls.

You pointed things out with your pen. 'You're trying to make a very sophisticated point here,' you told me. 'But you've got to make sure your text is sophisticated enough to carry it across.'

I was only half in your world. I was barking orders at my prisoners. Orders to kneel. Orders to lie down. 'Oh, okay,' I said, politely. I know I said it exactly as if I couldn't give a damn.

'You need to be more conscious of what each paragraph is meant to convey.'

'Oh, right.' Orders to submit. I smiled the special smile I kept for admonishments from teachers and my aunt and uncle: bright and competent.

'It has to consist of a series of points which lead to an inevitable conclusion.'

'Oh, all right. Sure.'

You looked me in the eyes, leaning back in your seat. 'You don't care, do you?'

'Not really,' I said airily.

Then I shifted uncomfortably, aware that I hadn't concentrated enough on my defences. I covered my embarrassment with a smile that was at once knowing and ingratiating. My private perversions itched at my mind.

You said, 'Well, you'd best go to lunch then.'

I went to lunch.

Like a low-pitched noise gradually rising in intensity, however, your presence in the world began to assert itself.

You lived near me. Like me, you preferred to walk home, at least when you didn't have too many teaching materials to carry.

I used to make my way home from school along a dirt path which cut through the road reserve that ran along behind my aunt and uncle's house. I liked the sense of solitude. It was like being in the bush. You could hear the cars on the highway, but you couldn't see them. There were no houses in view—both sides of the path were walled with thick, tangled bushes. They were virulent, introduced species, engaged in the gradual green wrestle of choking out the native plants.

Usually, of course, my thoughts were brimming frantically with ideas for tonight's session.

I was imagining a new picture to add to my collection.

That's why I started when you called, 'Hello there!'

I turned to face you.

You stood, a picture of apology, under a scarecrowish eucalyptus sapling. 'I didn't mean to scare you,' you said, palms forward, begging pardon. 'Sorry.'

I remembered myself, and answered with chummy sarcasm, 'No, *I'm* sorry. I didn't mean to jump.'

That made you chuckle.

'Do you live around here?' I asked, as we fell into a rhythm, walking side by side.

'I've moved in on Johnson Avenue. It's at the end of the path, and right, a few blocks.' Your face was spotted red with exertion.

Silence. Afterwards, in your red and black journal, you wrote in thick black ink, 'Idiot! Why didn't you talk to her properly? She was *bored*.'

I wasn't bored, of course, but distracted, thinking of the pencilled shapes of waists and thighs.

'Oh, right,' I said, noncommittally. My courteous face was armour against intrusion. My manners were a martial art.

'Where do you live, then?'

'Just down here.' I nodded forwards, towards the gateway to my backyard.

'Do you?'

I nodded, thinking of my sketchbooks.

Searching earnestly around for another topic of conversation, you told me, 'You know, your essay on Blake was very good.'

'Thanks.' We reached the tree behind which was the gate into my backyard. I stopped. 'This is where I get off.'

'Bye, then,' you said. 'Enjoy your evening.'

'Will do.' I said, and disappeared.

You stood there for a moment, your hands in your pockets, staring after me. I suppose you were thinking how endearing I was, in my funny alien way.

*

When I first met you, I was sixteen years old. I had been aware for some months of a gradually rising intensity in the nature of my fantasies, and in my reaction to them. Where, a year before, it would have been enough to make one of the characters bare her breasts to me, I now had to hurt them—I mean bruise them, I had to hear her cry out—to fulfil the same need.

I suppose I could just blame hormones. But it seemed to me at the time that I was somehow becoming badder, more depraved. I was falling further, every time I found myself alone, into the dark depths of my spirit.

My burden weighed more and more heavily on me. I felt ancient, twisted, withered.

My very youth came as a sharp surprise whenever I found myself confronted with it. I lived under such a constant weight of obsession that my smooth cheeks and brown baby's eyes in the bathroom mirror seemed a mask. The mirror thought me worried—and perhaps a little severe, with my plain yellowish-blonde ponytail and unpierced ears—but not evil. What a blatant deception!

I wasn't born innocent.

My instincts were vicious, predatory, from the start. When I met you, I had been a voyeur as long as I'd had eyes. My very reflexes were sadistic. The ascent of my reason from the animal ways of infanthood served only to give a form to my state, as a painter gives shape to a colour. It seemed I learned to think in order to fantasise.

Unformed wisps of violently coloured fantasy, dating from when I was six or seven, survive inside this adult mind. I remember sitting belted into the back of the car, on the way to or from some errand. My aunt and uncle were silent in the front. I stared out the window, and in my child's head I tied my friends up with skipping ropes from the sports cupboard. My heart beat wildly.

The victims were always my peers. In those days, I went to school with boys. In those days, there were boys in my fantasies.

My fantasies appeared before my conscience began to form. My secret attacks resulted from as natural an instinct as eating.

There were no mitigating circumstances.

There were no excuses.

The ideas were never inspired by anything.

Do you see, darling? It was my personal evil—nothing to do with any outside factors. I wasn't young and malleable and suffering from an overdose of Hannibal the Cannibal. I wasn't a victim of child sexual abuse. I didn't grow up in a civil war zone.

My uncle didn't beat me. I don't even have the excuse of neglect—I can't say he ignored me, either. If anything, he was faintly indulgent, though taciturn. I can clearly remember him letting me win at Scrabble every night for weeks when, at thirteen or so, I decided I liked the game.

I met you in town, once, when my aunt sent me in to buy bread and milk.

It was supposed to be winter, but the day was still and sunny. It was too hot, really, for a dufflecoat, but I wore one anyway, trying to ignore the damp patches under my arms. My sweaty hands twisted into tight fists, sunk deep in the pockets.

I hated walking past groups of boys my own age. Five or six of them, baggy-jeaned and boisterous, were hanging around outside a video arcade. When I heard them laugh, I felt mortified. I sizzled with embarrassment. I didn't even know if it was me they were laughing at, if my insignificance and paleness had attracted their derision (it must have, it must have— think how ridiculous I looked in that shop-window reflection, my mouth so laughably tight with the effort of trying to compose a mask of indifference with which to meet the world) or if I was, to them, like the passing buses. Just moving scenery, unworthy of comment.

You came out of the supermarket as I was passing, weighed down with shopping. I saw you first, standing directly in my path, and knew I'd have to speak to you.

'Heya,' I said.

'Oh ...' You fiddled about, transferring bags from one hand to the other, so that your burden was evenly distributed. 'How're you?'

'Oh, y'know.' Nearly mad with rage and unconsummateable, abstract desire. 'Can't complain.'

'Good. Good. Going shopping, are you?'

'Shopping? That's old news.' I displayed my plastic bag. 'Been there, done that.'

'I see. Do you, er? D'you want a lift home? I'm all finished here ...' You shrugged, as well as a man with three grocery bags on each wrist can shrug.

Inside my dufflecoat, my sweaty body told me tersely to accept. 'Yeah, that'd be great! Are you going now?'

You nodded.

I've read a passage in your diary, describing how intensely ludicrous you felt at that moment, how incapable of being interesting or charming, how your lower back ached faintly and you thought, 'I'm old. I'm old.'

'And is your car a limousine?' I wanted flippantly to know, as you set off and I came trotting at your heels.

'Well ... it all depends on your definition of limousine. If your definition of the word matches the actual car, then yes, it is a limousine.' Coughing apprehensively, you added, 'Semiotics, you see.'

'Excellent! Concepts and symbols, yeah?'

Nodding, you seemed very pleased. You were about to reply when I interrupted. 'So was it an expensive limousine?'

'Oh, yes. Nothing but the best.'

'A stretch one? One of those ones with a fridge full of champagne and a big video screen and velvet lounge chairs to sit on?'

'Mmmm.' You stopped by an ancient, weathered Fiat, fumbling in your pocket for the keys.

'Cool,' I said. Then I touched you for the first time, there on the pavement outside the newsagent's. ('Her skin was so incredibly soft,' you told your diary later. 'Her hands are those white little baby's hands, like the hands on porcelain dolls.') You couldn't seem to manage, with those bags braceleting your arm, to extract your car-keys from your trouser pocket. So I tried to take the bags off your right hand, but the handles had all twisted round, garrotting your wrist. I had to tug and tug, holding the bag handles in one hand and your arm in the other, to get them off. 'Sorry!' I said, laughing.

'That's all right,' you said, and you said it very quickly, your nervousness apparent.

In the car, you asked pointedly for directions, though I think you already knew the way. The yellow hairs on the backs of your hands were beaded with sweat. They shone in the afternoon sun.

In the passenger seat, I sat cross-legged, pointing out the quickest way through the few streets to my house.

It was too short a journey for conversation. I covered the silence by winding down my window and dabbling my fingers in the streaming air. I'd never done that before. I think I saw it in a movie. It felt weird: very cold, like running water. I wasn't sure I liked it.

At the bottom of my street, you asked me, 'Do you always sit like that?'

I answered, 'Yeah! Don't you?'

Your laugh seemed visceral, drawn from you by force. 'Wouldn't be able to reach the brakes.' I liked that, the sudden, explosive quality of it, the way it seemed to take you by surprise.

At my place, I grabbed my shopping and was out in a second. 'Thanks heaps!'

You stuttered, seemed about to ask me some further question. 'That's fine,' was what you managed, before driving off, ears burning.

One winter morning I walked through the mist to school. My stockinged ankles got wet from the ice-studded dew. The lane behind my house would have been eerie, all shrouded in cold smoke, except for the screech of nearby traffic.

There was quite a little crowd around the fence near the school bus stop. A schoolgirl rugby scrum, all backs curved inwards. They were all peering down, looking at something.

I'm human. I wanted to see. I scooted round to the side of the crowd, seeking entry.

I recognised your car straight away. It was parked in the street at a jerky, panicked angle.

'Yuck!' said Rachel, loudly.

'What's happening?' I asked her elbow. I couldn't see. I was too short.

'He's *touching* it! It's gross!'

All those tartan backs provoked me into a frenzy of curiosity.

'What is it?' No-one answered.

'Yuck! It's bleeding!' I heard, and: 'That is *so* foul!'

Scooting out into the gutter, I squeezed between Rachel and another girl, and along beside the car. Now I was, suddenly, on centre stage, in the middle of the half-moon of protesting girls.

I saw you, kneeling awkwardly on grass between the path and the road. You were surrounded by curtains and panels of red and white tartan, barred in by endless red-stockinged legs. From here, behind you, I could only see the arc of your back, suited in brown tweed, and the bottom of one shoe. You rested your backside on your ankle.

In a flash of movement, I saw blood gleaming dully on one of your hands. A chorus of disgust hummed out through the crowd.

'Sir! Gross!'

One girl flung her hands before her face.

'Just *leave* it!'

'Urck, he's getting it all over his *hands*!'

I heard a kind of whimper, a kind of quiet yowl. I thought for a second that you might have made the noise. Approaching closer, caught in the gravitational pull of curiosity, I sidled round in front of several taller girls.

And then I saw.

I saw that you were kneeling over some matted, blood-flecked creature that lay in the sandy mud. I saw your hands extended, literally at arm's length, as you tried to offer comfort without causing more pain.

At first, I thought it might be a rabbit. The fur was that dull rabbit pale brown, where it wasn't torn or stained.

Then it yowled again. You flinched away, wincing.

I saw the ears. 'Oh, it's a cat,' I said.

'Not for long!' said someone behind me.

It lay shivering, complaining feebly. Its head seemed to lie at a strange limp angle. Your hands were poised just above it, in an agony of uncertainty. A horrible flattened gash in the bottom of its stomach gave glimpses of brown visceral things.

'Sir, that is *disgusting*! Just leave it here.'

You wiped at your forehead distractedly, and, oh, my darling, you painted yourself with the cat's blood in the process. A long red-brown streak stretched across your temples. 'I can't just leave it here! It'll die!'

'It's gonna die anyway,' decided Rachel. She snapped her gum with finality.

In protest, the cat whined again, pumping a front paw weakly back and forth.

'Its eyes are weird,' said someone.

They were; all white and membranous, as though someone had stretched plastic bags over the irises.

People started to notice your forehead. A whispered giggle rippled through the crowd. You squatted like an incompetent Christ, garlanded with cat's blood. In the distance, the school bell rang out like a bomb siren.

'We should get a vet,' you said, patting the dying animal gingerly. It spasmed, mouth stretched open in a catastrophic yawn.

Rachel replied, 'We should go in.'

'I can't ... I can't quite pick it up.' You moved your hands towards its sides, through the mud, but flinched away from the raw surface of the wound at the last moment.

'*Don't* pick it up,' she ordered. 'It's foul.'

There were nods of agreement. Girls began to retreat towards the big iron-crested gates, staring behind with contempt and fascination.

'Just leave it,' said Rachel, and turned on her heel.

And there you were, within thirty seconds, a martyr, kneeling in the mud without even an audience.

I put my bag down in the gutter. I crouched beside you, putting down one hand to steady myself and muddying my palm.

'I'll pick it up ...' I said. 'If you drive.'

The look on your face was like wild hope.

Rachel and two stragglers saw me as they passed in through the gates. 'Just *leave* it!' she shouted once more, and was gone.

We worked efficiently together, you and I.

I bundled the cat, as best I could, onto an improvised plastic-bag stretcher, and then picked it up from underneath, scraping my hands through the mud in an effort to make the transition from the ground to the air as smooth as possible. The cat felt warm, even through the plastic. It mewed pathetically, working one paw in the air, trying feebly to knock away its pain.

'Hop in, hop in!' you told me, wrenching open the door for me like a fumbling chauffeur. Jumping into the driver's seat, you asked breathlessly, 'D'you know where there's a vet?'

'Yep,' I said confidently. Something warm and wet was leaking into my lap. 'Near the dentist's. Up from the supermarket. We used to take our cat there.' Before it was run over.

'Right,' you said, hunching forwards with concentration. As we pulled away, I realised that you were doing your best to drive smoothly, so as not to cause the cat any more pain than was necessary. As we rounded the corner, you needed to know: 'How's he doing? Do you think he'll be all right?'

The animal had stopped whimpering, and lay panting gutturally, its face averted. Something sopped through my uniform and ran in droplets down between my thighs. 'Yeah, he'll be all right,' I assured you. 'He just needs to be stitched up.'

'I didn't see him,' you explained, accelerating down a wide empty street. 'I just felt this *bump*!'

'It's okay,' I said. 'It can happen to anyone.'

'I hope he isn't in too much pain. I didn't see him.'

'It's just down this street. On the left there.'

We found a park easily. 'Thank God for that!' You jumped out and slammed your door emphatically, before running around the car to yank mine open.

We took our pathetic, dripping bundle into the vet's waiting room.

The receptionist—an overweight, middle-aged, well-meaning woman—was impressed by your sense of urgency, and called the vet over the intercom.

The vet was a small pointy man with wire-rimmed glasses. He opened his surgery door to its full extent, and stood in the doorway like a portrait in a frame, his arms folded. 'Yes?' he said.

'He's been run over!' you said, hustling the man and me and the cat back through the door of the surgery.

You shook the little man's hand, uncertainly, and he looked down in sudden acute distaste at the mess of congealed blood which he took away with him.

On the operating table, the vet unwrapped our unsavoury parcel, and eyed the broken cat. 'She'll have to be put down, I think,' he murmured. 'Is she yours?'

You shook your head as the vet drew an efficient syringe. 'No, I don't know whose he is. I just felt this *bump*, and I stopped straight away ...'

'He hasn't got a collar,' I said. 'He could be anyone's.'

'Oh, dear. Poor old thing,' soothed the vet with the solicitude of habit, injecting colourless death beneath the quaking animal's chin. 'Poor old girl.'

Almost immediately, the animal was still. 'There,' said the vet, wiping his hand on his white coat. 'She won't feel any more pain now. There's not much you can do, when they're like that.'

Moving your mouth soundlessly, you seemed to be trying to ask a question.

'Don't worry,' said the vet. 'We'll dispose of her.'

Walking out through the reception room, we must have looked an insane pair, my only darling. The blood across your forehead was dry and flaking, like garish facepaint. One of your hands was smudged all over with it, as though you'd been busy ripping the entrails out of sheep. I wore an apron of the stuff, a dark spreading stain across my lap.

In the car, there were spots the size of twenty-cent pieces on the passenger's seat. An unpleasant metallic smell hung so heavily in the air that I could taste it as I breathed.

You drove in silence, at first, staring straight ahead with the acute concentration of the shock victim.

I sat beside you, being cold.

As we rounded the corner into the school's street, you told me, 'It's my fault. I just didn't see him.'

Standing inside the school gates, you at last noticed my ruined uniform.

'Oh, you've got it all over your *dress*!' You looked visibly upset. 'I'm so sorry ... I didn't even see. Look, come along to the sick bay. We'll fix you up.'

I stood like a discarded meat tray outside the front office, while you charmed the po-faced woman who administered the clothing pool into lending me another uniform for the day, and giving me a new pair of stockings. Passing girls running messages for teachers looked at me with derision, imagining a menstrual disaster.

In the sick-bay toilet, with an ancient flannel and a deeply crevassed rock of soap, I cleaned myself up as best I could. For some reason, I wasn't at all disgusted at the thought that a cat had bled on me.

When I came out—cleaner, dressed in a stiff new uniform— I found you waiting for me.

With a funny combination of formality and sentiment, you said, 'I really appreciate what you did.'

There was a catch in your voice. Leaning against the starch-white wall, you thrust your hands into your jacket pocket. There was a spot of blood on your lapel.

'That's all right,' I said, brightly.

I didn't look at your face. I counted the buttons on your shirt.

Now that the immediacy of action was over, you made me uncomfortable. Oh, not for the reasons you might suspect, darling! I still hadn't the faintest idea how you felt about me. It didn't even occur to me that you had an ulterior reason for crossing your legs the way you did. It was just that your sheer, instinctive *humanity* overwhelmed me with guilt and regret and frustration.

'I'm sorry about your dress.'

I laughed. 'I don't care about the dress! Horrible thing. I hate wearing it.'

Relieved, you pressed: 'You're sure?'

I nodded through you, at the wall.

I didn't yet realise that this humanity of yours was something I could *use*. It loomed like a murder next door—compelling, close, discomfiting. But still, at this stage, someone else's business.

'Still,' you said, walking me to the door, your hands clasped together, monk-like, in front of you, 'at least he didn't suffer.' You opened the door for me.

'Yeah,' I said. 'At least, not any more than was necessary.'

At home, I sat cross-legged on my bed, sketchbook open, drawing furiously. I drew Rachel, with angry, lewd strokes. I made her naked before me. Omnipotent, I wreaked vengeance with a pencil.

As the afternoon melted into evening, I drew her kneeling, her forehead touching the ground, her arms pinned together behind her back. Her hair was dishevelled, about to escape the loose bun at the back of her head. Tendrils snaked, Medusa-like, around her ears. Her eyes were closed in pain. Her mouth was parted slightly, as though she were exhausted. I drew the long luxurious curve of her naked back with satisfaction. My eyes narrowed as I sketched in her buttocks and her legs, curled anyhow under her, as though she had been pushed to the ground with force and was too weary and dispirited even to fall comfortably.

I was defending you, darling. I was punishing her for her derision, her harsh voice and mocking smile.

The abuse of your kindness enraged me. My heart raced, thinking of that scornful crowd of vixens, watching you, laughter curling their lips, as you watched the cat, tears stinging your eyes.

My homework lay neglected at the bottom of my schoolbag. The light all drained away from my window, but I didn't switch the lamp on. I sat there, still and silent, as my white hands in my lap turned royal blue, then purple. I was watching the tortured image before me melt away into the darkness.

The next day, as I was walking through the teachers' carpark, your car pulled up, in a flurry of gravel, almost next to me.

'Heya,' I said.

'Oh ...' You looked flustered as you slammed the car door. 'Oh, hello.' Fumbling with the boot of the car, you asked, 'Your—er—parents weren't too upset about the dress, were they?'

Ignoring your faux pas, I said : 'Nah. I soaked it. It all came out.'

'Still—' You were extracting piles of manila folders and hugging them awkwardly to your chest as you shut the boot— 'you should be proud of what you did.'

'Yeah, I am.' On tiptoes, I reached up to your stack of folders, and took the top third for myself.

'Oh.' You went bright red. 'Thank you very much, m'dear.'

I liked 'm'dear'. It had a slightly foppish ring to it which matched your endless supply of baggy-trousered tweed suits and your hair that hung in two lank flops. It was exotic, too; with an aroma of some strange English spice that fascinated me, used to smelling only the overwhelming chemical scent of spray deodorant on my body.

I trotted along at your heels. I liked the way you strode along, like a flamingo on important business.

As we entered the building, Kara came out. You nodded politely at her. 'Morning,' you said.

'Hi,' she said. I felt her blue eyes burning into my back as I followed you inside.

After we'd entered your classroom and dumped the folders on your desk, you thanked me earnestly. As I turned to go, you said cheerily, 'Well … I'll see you in class after lunch, won't I?'

'Yep!' I said.

I sat and read through Maths. The myopic supply teacher never noticed.

By recess, rumours about my blood-stained uniform of the day before had reached my friends.

Walking through the stark concrete quadrangle, Laura wanted to know: 'Did you have a little *accident*, yesterday?'

This was the sort of scene I had been dreading for years. Heart-sunk, soul-scuttled, I turned to answer her. But now that the worst had happened, and I was unmasked as a freak, I did find a sort of stony pride to face her down with.

'What?' I sounded irritable, busy, as though I had other things on my mind.

'I heard there was blood all over you.'

'Cat's blood,' I answered with terse truthfulness, ducking into the hallway.

I don't know if she believed me.

But from then on, my friends carefully distanced them-selves. They said 'Hi' to me in the locker room, but then turned pointedly away to focus on more important conversations. They neglected to invite me to parties and withheld juicy bits of gossip.

It was only to be expected. I knew I'd done wrong. I'd been *weird*. I'd sided with a teacher—a weird teacher, at that: one who made a stupid, laughable attempt to make himself likable—against Rachel and the group. But it still stung to be so suddenly declared unclean, unfit to associate with, when I'd worked so hard to fit in.

I spent some weeks as an outcast, hovering lunchtimes away in the library or under distant trees.

My fury at my friends was vague and generalised. They were all guilty, as a crowd. Quietly, methodically, I went about the business of drawing exactly what I thought of them.

I filled half a sketchbook, that week. Agitation kept me awake, long into the silences of the night.

By Friday, discussions of weekend plans that flagrantly didn't include me had taunted me into an agony of restlessness. I ran home, through a sudden drizzle, kicking at stones, ripping the leaves from trees and shredding them with my fingers.

I couldn't eat my dinner. Too many shapes—too much skin—came crowding in on my senses. There was no room for food. I made an excuse and retreated to my room.

I suppose I must have seemed strained and distant enough to worry my aunt and uncle.

I suppose that's why, after I thought he was in bed, my uncle came and tapped at my door.

I suppose that's why, when I didn't answer, he opened the door and entered.

I had crept along the corridor to the toilet. On the way back, I heard nothing except the rain swishing against the ground outside.

I remember seeing my uncle leaning over my sketchbooks, his arms straight, his hands curled under the edge of the desk. I must have touched the door slightly. The hinges creaked, and he spun around in an instant, like a matador.

His face was maroon with fury. Lumps like cellulite sprang up in his forehead. He strode across the floor towards me, pulling himself up to his full height.

I cowered.

'What is this?' he demanded, thrusting his big body even closer to mine. I felt the cold smooth plaster of the wall against my back. I couldn't retreat any further. Across the room, I could see my pencil sketches lying bare to the air, open to any eye. I was struck anew by the careful lewdness, the clinical perversion, of the subject matter.

I started to shake. I was a criminal engaged in a complicated felony. I had been found out and I would be punished.

He lunged for me, his face swollen, eyes bulging hideously.

'What are they?' He grabbed me with both hands. His fingers dug painfully in below my collarbones. In retrospect, I think there was a kind of panic on his face, a frantic uncertainty, as though, having caught me by the shoulders, he was uncertain what to do with me.

I couldn't say anything. Hot hysteria crept through my veins, flushing my face and neck. I shook my head, more to deny the situation than the crime.

His voice was shrill. His moustache convulsed, caterpillar-like.

'Did you draw them? *Did you?*' I could feel his breath

gusting over my face.

I gave a spastic nod, closing my eyes so I didn't have to look at his ferocious, hostile face.

Fury condensed in his hands. He shook me violently. 'They're disgusting!'

I knew that. Of course they were disgusting.

'What kind of—' he wanted to know.

I didn't know what kind of teenage girl had files full of detailed sadistic fantasies, either. I trembled in his grasp.

'You're an animal!' Again, the hands contracted, vice-like. This time he lifted me completely off the ground, banging me back down like a sack of potatoes.

An ancient reptilian panic awoke in me. I started to struggle, to writhe and bend. He gripped me more tightly than ever, making a fan of fingertip-shaped bruises across each shoulder.

The redness in my face overflowed into snivelling tears. They ran down my cheeks in an uneven stream. I snorted violently, wriggling every second.

'You're an *animal*!' he said, right in my ear this time. I turned my head, opened my mouth, and confirmed his accusation by sinking my teeth into his wrist.

'Shit!'

He let go instantly, clapping one hand over his wound. I didn't wait to see what would happen. I turned and fled, bumping down the dark stairs, sobbing incoherently. I fought with the deadlock on the front door till the cold metal bit into my hands, and flew, finally, out into the night.

I came pelting, I came pounding. All the dogs of hell were on my tail. I couldn't see a thing. I ran with one hand up to shield my eyes, as though I were running into a dazzling light.

Great sluglike droplets of rain collected on the leaves above and then unleashed themselves on me, like waterbombs. My little tears were all flooded away.

It was a low treacherous undergrowth that I ran through, stumbling on roots, catching my foot on traitorously curved low branches, bruising myself on treetrunks. I cried out in frustration when I fell onto my face. The mud sucked at my knees and elbows. It didn't want to let me stand again, but I dragged myself to my feet, lurching onwards, blindly.

I didn't know where I was going. I just crashed on through.

It was just luck that I ended up on the avenue.

I didn't realise where I was, not for a few seconds. I only knew that the leaves and the sticks, the clutching witch's fingers, no longer barred my way. I folded my arms and lowered my head and charged onwards.

There was asphalt under my feet and a fine spray of rain on my face. I yelped when my calf dragged against something sharp.

I hopped for a few steps. I'd cut my leg. The cold rain stung the wound. I didn't care.

I ran and I ran. The streetlights made weak puddles of light, which I avoided instinctively.

I wasn't looking for your house. When I saw a looming dark ark to my left, some beast's instinct told me to seek shelter there. I must have recognised your car parked in the driveway.

And that's how you found me, doubled over as though I'd been punched, hammering hysterically on your door with one muddy fist.

A light went on somewhere away behind the door, and then it was open. Light flooded out all over me, and you stood there, the silhouette of an angel.

'Oh, my God!' you said. Or something like that.

I couldn't speak.

You took me by one wrist and led me inside.

I was, suddenly, in some kind of beige haven, with soft gentle carpet underfoot and a reassuring sofa in the corner. There were tribal artifacts arrayed on some of the shelves, and books on others. Totem masks with big hollow eyes stared down from the walls.

I'd woken you up, of course. You were still blinking away sleep. Your hair was *everywhere*. You'd thrown on a T-shirt and a pair of boxer-shorts.

What I mostly remember is you holding me gently at arm's length, one hand on each shoulder. You stood in front of me, just peering down intently into my face, with your big green eyes.

I had snot running down my chin. I was still shuddering with fear and strange hiccupping tears. I was conscious, now, of being very cold. I was all covered in little stings and aches. You seemed to sense this, and propelled me over to the sofa and sat me down.

Turning away, you found a tissue and wiped my face carefully. The tissue quickly became sodden with rainwater and tears and snot. You screwed it up into a ball and dropped it unceremoniously on the floor. Then you wiped, very tenderly, at the corners of my eyes with one finger.

'What's happened?' There was a reddening at the corners of your eyes, and a fine glaze of tears.

I must have looked pretty pathetic. You must have thought I'd been the victim of an assault.

I couldn't say a word.

I tried to speak, and couldn't. I let out one frenzied sob. I sucked the next sob in, with a slurping noise. I wiped my eyes with the back of one hand.

'Oh, you poor little ...' Your face split open with pity.

Then you did a strange thing. You took my wet teary hand in your two hands, and you pressed it to your lips. You inhaled deeply through your nose, and gave a sort of angry sigh. 'Come on.'

When I didn't move, you stood up, and replaced my hand carefully into my lap, like a man returning a valuable item he has been lent. 'We'd better get you cleaned up.'

And then you picked me up, one hand under my knees and the other behind my neck, the way a father picks up a sleepy toddler. It was such a relief not to have to *run* anywhere any more, to let my tired legs dangle uselessly over your arm. Your skin on mine felt hot. I shivered. My leg hurt.

'You're freezing!' you said, as we went off down the hall. Passing under the hall light, I scrunched my eyes shut, dizzy with distress. I had a headache.

When I opened my eyes again, we were in a bathroom where everything was bottle-green or gleaming white. It was very clean and smelled of aftershave. You sat me on a wicker basket (it must have been your dirty-laundry basket) and stroked my face and arms and muddy legs with a hot wet flannel. Spots of blood dimpled the white floor. They smudged across the flannel as you moved it.

Exhausted, I leant my head on the towel rail. Grabbing a green towel, you proceeded to pat dry my arms and legs. You said, 'I'm going to get you some of my pyjamas. I want you to take *this* off.' You tugged significantly at the hem of my uniform. It was filthy. Soaking wet, splodged with mud and spattered, near the bottom, with tiny droplets of my blood.

I stood up as you left, and obeyed. I had to tug quite hard to get the obstinate, clinging thing over my head. Instinctively, I turned my back on the mirror.

In a few moments, you returned with some blue flannel pyjamas, looking at the floor as you handed them to me.

I got dressed. You stood with your arms folded and your back to me, a determined gentleman. When you turned around, you smiled.

'I think you might need to roll those up a bit. Here.' Kneeling down, you rolled the sleeves up and up, until you could see my hands. Then you bent right down, your broad back level with my knees, and did the same with the legs, until my pale scratched feet were exposed to the air.

Racked with tiny after-sobs, I smiled wanly.

You squatted by me. I saw the white arches of your bare feet. 'Now,' you said carefully, looking into my face, 'have you got anywhere you can go tonight?'

I shook my head.

Carefully still, you asked, 'Do you want to stay here?'

I supposed so. I nodded.

'All right then. Come on.'

As though I were blind, you walked behind me, one hand on each arm, guiding me. We went awkwardly up the stairs and into a bedroom.

'This is the spare room,' you explained. 'My brother and his wife sleep here, when they come.'

There were cardboard boxes in rows on the floor, flaps open, spouting books. Against the window there was a double bed, like a display in a bedding shop. You tugged back the covers until a welcoming triangle of sheet showed. 'Hop in.'

I did, sinking back onto the piled pillows. Gently, you

covered me up, pressing the blankets down against my shoulder.

There was a wicker-backed chair by the foot of the bed. Yanking it across the floor, you planted yourself by my head.

Clearing your throat, you said, 'Right.' You sat by my bed like a man constrained by an uncomfortable duty. You were restless. Your knees jigged up and down, up and down. I saw the dense yellow hairs foresting over your thighs.

'Something's obviously...' You nodded at me, at my battered self. 'Well, you wouldn't be...'

I watched you wrestle with words and then speak in plastic banalities. These cliches, you hauled painfully up out of the depths of your concern.

To me, a fugitive in someone else's pyjamas, they seemed like jewels.

You battled yourself, a man wrestling a boa constrictor. You forced your eyes on me.

Like a man confessing his sins, you said, 'In some ways I wish you hadn't come here ... to me, alone like this.'

You stammered: 'I mean, I coucoucouldn't ever hurt you ...' Then: 'If I find out who's hurt you, I'll bloody well kill them!'

So then you felt obliged to explain yourself: 'I've always liked you, ever since I met you ... You seem like a pretty amazing girl.'

Silence.

It wasn't enough. Your scruples demanded a clearer revelation. Your voice tore on 'very' when you said, 'You're a very beautiful girl.'

I saw you squirming before me like a insect pinned to cardboard.

My darling, such an appeal to my vanity was impossible to

ignore. I saw your midnight bird's-nest hair, and those big eyes, and nervous fingers.

A new desire woke in me. *I wanted you.*

I wanted you at that moment, when I understood how desperately you wanted me. I wanted you when I saw how you dreaded to touch me, fearing me broken. When I saw you pinching violently at the skin of your own wrist, leaving an angry red weal. I recognised the gesture. I'd done that to myself, trying to distract myself from the images I made.

It seemed to me that you were punishing yourself for the most innocent of passions. You were charmingly, naively presuming yourself guilty of lechery, debauchery, debasement. *How could you have the faintest clue?* It was laughable that you should be parading your shame before me—a good man like you.

So I, newly sainted, newly made innocent, reached for that agitated pinching right hand of yours, and I took it in mine.

'Thank you so much,' I said. The words and the gratitude were sincere. The virtuous big eyes I made were not; or at least they did not occur naturally. I put them there. 'I really appreciate you doing ... all this—'

'Oh, don't be stupid!' you pooh-poohed me. I had every right, it seemed, to expect your help.

'No, I ... it means a lot to me.' The back of your hand glowed with blond down. I stroked it gently, with my thumb. Your hand tightened involuntarily around mine. It was almost a spasm. '*You* mean a lot to me.'

Dismissing my affections as unnecessary, you exclaimed, 'Oh, be quiet!'

'No.' I was a petulant little girl, with her lower lip protruding. 'I do ...' I made the easy declaration seem difficult, pretending to fumble for words that were readily available, '... care about you too. I really do.' Big eyes again.

I saw you swallow, a snake gulping a guinea pig. You didn't take your hand back. Instead you left it to sweat gently on mine.

This was the moment. Biting my lip, making my face tentative, I asked out of the blue, 'Will you kiss me?'

You jumped as though stung. 'Oh!' It could have been a gasp of physical pain, or surprise, or shock. Flustered, you shook your head; let your hair flop down over your face; avoided my gaze. But you betrayed yourself: you did not snatch your hand away. You left yourself in my grasp.

'Please?' The little girl, saccharine, insisted upon her own way.

With a deep breath and a saint's stern gathering of composure, you explained: 'It wouldn't be right ... There are some things a teacher and a student just *can't* ... however he might feel ... however *I* might feel ...' Your voice was level, but I saw your knees quake. I saw you tighten your legs, bend forward—oh, so slightly—to hide your erection.

I dug about for your pity. 'Don't you fancy me?'

You exhaled by way of a laugh, shaking your head: 'Oh, my *dear girl*—' savouring those words, as though often in your mind you had said them to me—'*you have no idea.*' And you shook your head again.

With one swift flowing movement, like a snake doing ballet, I knelt up, so as to have my face close to yours.

You would not look at me. You kept very still. Your breath shivered in and out. I put my fingertips against your cheek. You yielded under the tiniest pressure, and turned to face me.

I crouched tense, a predator in the long grass. Once I had

your eyes in mine, you were my creature. You couldn't hide your passion—indeed, you presented it to me, showed me with your face: *This is how much I want you.* Your eyes, seeing me, shouted, *Oh, please!* I coasted forwards, and in a single long, smooth motion, placed my lips on yours.

You yelped—then surrendered. Kissed me back, hot mouth on mine, tremulous breath on my tongue. Then wrenched your head backwards, away, shaking it from side to side in slow bewilderment.

I didn't pursue you. Your face was stark, panicked, your eyebrows knotted together in terror. 'We can't,' you said. 'We mustn't.'

I hoped your scruples were not so strong in you that you'd relinquish me. I worried that you'd leap to your feet, run from the room, slamming the door behind you. You dug your top teeth into your bottom lip, shaking your head. Your face was red.

'I'm sorry. Have I embarrassed you?'

But none of this was my fault. 'Don't be silly ... it's me,' you told me gently. I gazed at you, eyes wide, lips a sensuous half-inch open, suddenly aware of the marvellous, theatrical effect of the tear streaks on my cheeks, the blood-red scratches on my thin hands. You saw all this, and I saw you melt. Looking old, filled with pity, you said, 'Oh, you poor little thing, you should be able to come to someone for help without him ...'

'What?'

'*I'm* sorry,' you said, firmly.

I played an ace, and started to cry.

I wasn't hysterical; not hiccuping with anguish, as I had been when you opened the door to me. I shot you a look of distress, confusion, loneliness, abandonment, and let the water come sliding down my cheeks.

These silent, helpless tears left you no choice but to swivel your body to face me, to come closer, to put your arms awkwardly around me.

'Come here. Come on. It's okay. It's all right. I've got you. Don't cry.'

I put one hand on your shoulder and buried my face in your neck, trembling with tears. 'Don't cry. It's okay. Don't cry.'

You rested your chin on the top of my head. I sensed that you were savouring that touch, my soft hair against your face. I took a deep, shuddering, sorrowful breath. Pulling back, turning my face up to look at yours, I wiped my eyes impatiently with the heel of my hand, and begged to know: 'Don't you like me?'

'Of course I like you!'

'But you don't fancy me?'

Silence. Your hands tensed against my back. 'I do,' you admitted, levelly.

I grinned for joy through my tears. 'Well, that's okay then!'

'No, my dear, it isn't—'

'Please?' Leaning forward, I kissed your cheek affectionately. 'Please?'

You took a breath, looking for a moment as though you were trying to frame complex, rational arguments in your mind. You wanted to spout pros and cons, tick things off on your fingers. Then, with a funny, tragic little half-smile, you brushed the fingers of one hand down my cheek.

Again, we kissed. You slid your hand onto my neck. We kissed like proper lovers. I pressed close into you. I liked the feel of your warm body.

I wanted your hand on my breast. I reached behind, took your hand, showed it. 'Oh, darling—' you said, your hand hovering half an inch above—'are you sure?'

'Yep,' I confirmed, fiddling with the unfamiliar pyjamas. Forcing them through the holes, I delicately wrenched the top two buttons open. My small breasts were there, just below the flannelette. I took your hand again, and introduced them. 'Is that nice?'

You cupped my breast, your cheeks ticking with the effort of your surrender.

Seeing the fresh-red five-fingered bruises on my collarbones, you whined, 'Oh, angel ...'

'It's all right.' I was Orphan Annie, dismissing my difficulties with a grin. 'Come on,' I said, shuffling over, patting the bed beside me. 'Please?'

Snorting with disbelief, you complied, sliding, a little awkwardly, beneath the sheets.

Now that we were two bodies in the same medium, so to speak, you abandoned yourself to the experience.

I lay on my back, and you propped yourself on your elbows above me, looking down. Your body seemed to understand mine, to mirror its actions through the activity of some force as natural as gravity. When I wriggled free of my clothes, a snake shedding her skin, you did the same without a word. We ejected our clothing onto the floor.

Big-eyed, you touched me so delicately it tickled.

Your lips closed around my nipple and it felt warm, reassuring. You touched my thighs lightly, with the whole inside of your hand. You stroked the curve between my hip and my underarm.

'Is that ... nice?' You blushed, smiling a little, ruefully, at your own discomfort.

'It's lovely.'

'Are you sure you want to—'

'Yes! You boring man! Stop asking me that!'

'I can't believe this.' You were staring at me, amazed.

The ghost of a thousand American movies made me say, as I kissed you briefly, fiercely, on the mouth, 'Believe it!'

You found in my nakedness a miracle, a sacred trust.

I found yours very interesting.

I had never seen adult male genitalia, and I told you so.

'Well?' you wanted to know, squinting with embarrassment and delight. 'What d'you reckon?'

I was surprised by all the hair. Reaching below the covers, I touched your penis, tentatively. I saw your eyes close, your mouth twitch, helpless as my hand closed around it.

'It's very silky,' I whispered, without letting go.

You nodded, and said with an effort, 'If you want to stop—'

'I don't want to stop.'

'... *just say so*. I won't be. I don't expect.'

Lifting the blankets, I peered down, intrigued, at the seat of your desire. 'Balls are bigger than I thought.'

In the midst of your profound discomfort, you laughed. 'Are they?'

'Can I touch?'

'Be very gentle.'

I touched. The sacks of skin in which they hung were wrinkly, prickly with hair. 'They're like eyeballs,' I pronounced with childish solemnity, cupping one carefully. 'Or mushy eggs.'

Your skin seemed to tremble around your flesh. 'Are they just?'

Sitting up, I pulled the covers back, doubling them over our legs. As I bent forward, you explored my spine with one heavy finger.

'You're so *little*,' you told me, approvingly.

I nestled back down beside you, my face a few inches below yours, my toes against your calves. 'You're so big.'

We lay for ages, side by side. Your hips moved backwards and forwards. Your face above your body was strained, abashed at the antics going on down below.

It's funny, isn't it? I'd never once fantasised about having sex with a man, yet I knew what to do by instinct. I knew where to touch you and when to kiss you, even though all of this was completely foreign to my experience, alien to my imagination.

Gradually—I forget quite how, it all blurs into a general impression of milky skin and fuzzes of hair—I found myself underneath you. You balanced on straight arms. Your face was a foot from mine, but I could feel your breath hot on my fore-head, as though I'd opened an oven.

You said, red-faced, 'You're sure, aren't you?'

I felt your penis at the door, a strange bulbous stem.

'Oh—I don't want to hurt you.'

It seemed like something far too big to ever fit inside.

'Don't worry.' I pulled my legs right up, my knees by my ears.

Closing your eyes, fumbling with one hand—I felt your curled fingers against my thigh, very high up—you forced yourself inside.

And with that thrust, you dealt the death-blow to those battalions of tortured bodies in my mind. The chains fell from their wrists and ankles. They pulled on cloaks and walked out of me, away into the night.

Your eyes were closed. I winced. Withdrawing, you opened your eyes, and watched my face as you came sliding back in. I smiled, biting the inside of my lip surreptitiously.

'I'm trying to be gentle,' you told me, anxiously. 'Does it hurt?'

'No,' I lied, smiling wider, patting your forehead affectionately with my child's hands. 'It's *lovely.*'

My hands on your broad back enjoyed the sweat that welled there.

My ears enjoyed your laboured breathing, the little grunted half-words that broke from your throat against your will.

My eyes, turning downwards, feasted on the sight of your stomach, as it tensed and scrunched itself repeatedly, shivering down towards my flat belly, then gathering itself away, pulling back for another approach.

Your face was bestial, lips drawn back over your teeth in a chimpanzee's grimace of aggression. Shifting rednesses beneath your skin grew and burst like supernovas. And your eyes were bright like bits of glass with the sun shining through them.

'I love you,' you hissed between your teeth. You lowered your head onto my shoulder, your breath like fire in my ear. '*I love you!*'

I wondered how long this usually took.

More desperate now, you raised your head, arching back your neck, breathing like a horse. I felt a new, stiffened determination pulsing inside me.

On either side of my face, the insides of your arms were streaked with coiling tendons, bulging veins.

I stretched my arms above my head, showing you my chest more clearly. You gasped, shaking your head, and bit your lip.

With fascination, I watched your face. It was you who was incoherent now. It was you who were helpless and speechless and without hope. Faster you slammed into me and faster, impotent before the urgency of your body's demands.

At last, you tensed and shuddered and your eyes went wide and glazed like a dead man's. You seemed to flutter and fall, your big body deflating down over mine, melting onto me, welding itself to my skin.

I presumed that was the end.

Your collapse left your curly head on my shoulder. I could feel your hot fast breath blowing over my breasts.

I said, tenderly, 'Oh, you *darling*.' Snaking my arms beneath yours, I folded them around your exposed back. Enclosing you like that felt so primordially right that I almost giggled with triumph. Controlling myself, I pressed my lips against the crown of your head.

As though it were bowed down by a great weight, you lifted your head.

Looking up at me—looking *up*, from your reduced condition—you told me: 'Oh.'

In a forlorn gesture of compassion, reaching down between our four legs, you patted my pubic hair softly. 'I've hurt you, haven't I?' You looked worried and upset and helpless.

'Don't be silly.' I reassured you. I did feel sort of scraped—grated-up—inside, and there was a sharp stinging pain like a deep papercut where my legs met, which throbbed with every beat of my heart. But this evaporated into nothing beside the steady, reassuring weight of your body on mine.

'Am I squashing you?'

'No.'

'I must be heavy!'

'It's all right.'

'Are you sure?'

'*Yes!* You're like a blanket.'

'I must have hurt you.' There was a film of moisture, brought on by pity, glazing your exhausted eyes. 'I'm so sorry.'

I said, 'It's all right. It's all right.'

Comforting you against my pain, I knew that it was I who was old and weary and corrupt. I knew that you were the child.

Lying on your stomach, one of your hands cupped over one of mine, you wove in and out of sleep. Several times, I heard you forget yourself and begin to breathe raspingly, unconsciously, but I found that the slightest involuntary movement of my hand under yours prompted a reassuring 'I'm still here' squeeze of your fingers. You stroked my wrist with your index finger. Your warm hip nudged against mine, that sticky contact undulating with each breath either of us took.

I lay tensed with strangeness, remembering you as you were half an hour before, powerless before the onslaught of— as it seemed to me—an uncontrollable madness. Beside me, your skin a gentle gold in the lamplight, you began gently to snore.

When I woke up, I was alone. There was a rumpled look to the sheets next to me. They seemed compressed, dimpled. They were warm and they smelt faintly of sweat, in a comforting way.

I'd never slept naked before. The smooth cotton against my skin felt good. I wriggled luxuriously.

I couldn't hear you. I hoped you hadn't panicked and run off somewhere, leaving me to face the morning alone.

I dressed quickly in the pyjamas I'd worn the night before. It was cold. The sky beyond the window was still festooned with the shreds of last night's storm.

Afraid to stomp in your churchlike house, I tiptoed out the door (turning the handle gently, slowly, silently) and along the corridor.

I used the toilet, and found a long bright smear of blood on the toilet paper. I assessed the damage, and found no great cause for worry. It stung a little, but on the whole I didn't feel too bad.

Flushing the toilet to announce my approach, I headed down the stairs.

You sat, all dressed, at the glass-topped dining table, reading the newspaper.

'Heya,' I said. 'Is there any breakfast?'

There was a miserable edge to you, though you smiled widely in welcome. Mournful-eyed, you said, 'There's cornflakes. Or toast. You can have some muesli if you like.' You didn't meet my gaze. You were shadowed with worry, outlined in edginess.

I wondered if this was a one-night stand dismissal. Measured against the holy intensity of the night before, your standoffishness seemed very odd.

In the kitchen alone I fixed myself breakfast. In the lounge room with you I ate it in silence. I sat chewing, a demure two places away from you. I swung my legs back and forward. You didn't look up once from your paper. The cornflakes turned to cardboard in my mouth.

I was deathly afraid that you didn't want me.

Finishing my food and laying down my spoon, I said, 'Do you want me to go?'

Your answer was too quick. It overlapped with mine. 'I think you'd better. Come on.' And you led me upstairs again.

We stood in the bedroom, our dishevelled nest still unmade, the faint salty whiff of sex rising from the sheets. The space between us seemed to echo with emptiness. I didn't quite know where to put my body. I sat it on the foot of the bed, out of harm's way. Standing alone, you seemed stooped, diminished, bowed down by a terrible weight.

I wanted to feel sorry for you, but I didn't know where I stood.

'Now...' you murmured, avoiding my eye. 'What are we going to dress you in?'

'I can wear my uniform,' I suggested helpfully, hugging myself.

'It was filthy. I put it in the washing machine. It's still wet.' In the end, you loaned me jeans, a T-shirt, and a grey cardigan. Everything was far too big for me.

At the doorstep, I turned and kissed you on the cheek.

'Thanks for everything,' I said lightly, willing you to make some declaration, tell me how you felt, tell me what was going to happen.

You said nothing, strangled by guilt. There were tears on your cheeks and fear in your eyes. You squeezed my hand and, snatching it to your mouth, kissed it fiercely, silently declaring everything: *I love you, but we can't, we can't...*

You slammed the door—so you thought—on your One True Love, and went to do the crossword, your heart breaking.

My heart sang with certainty.

Walking home, I was conscious of a palpable absence.

In the winter cold of my small bedroom, I used to sit with my back against the wall and my knees raised over the central-heating grate, letting the warm air gradually bake my legs. The temperatures were set by my uncle. They were not mean; I didn't freeze. Nevertheless I was conscious, whenever the heat shuddered and wavered and died, of a middle-class moderation; an economy where I would have preferred excess. So it was with this sudden deletion of your hands from my waist and my hips, the vast expanse of your warmth from my side.

The fact that, as far as home life went, I had nothing left to me, soon became painfully obvious. My aunt and uncle simply withdrew themselves from me; turned from solid presences into vague whispering abstracts: a distant slamming of doors; a television murmuring to itself in another room; faint smells of aftershave and garlic lingering in the air. I could have been the only live being in a houseful of phantoms. Every space I stepped into seemed newly vacated.

Throughout that interminable weekend, we managed ourselves so that I didn't once set eyes on either my aunt or my uncle. I might as well have been a leper, shuffling around, cowled, waving a bell to warn of my approach.

I stayed in my room as much as possible, dreaming the hours away.

You owned carved trunks of dark, deeply waxed wood. Strange angular sculptures marched along the shelves. Antique books with mysterious inscriptions sat in orderly rows. It was like a museum. Or a chapel. It made me feel reverent.

Everything in your house seemed beautiful to me. It was a rare, exotic world; a whole other aesthetic. I wanted terribly to belong to it. I thought it would free me from the faded linoleum and bright plastic mugs of my upbringing.

I went downstairs once or twice, to use the bathroom and to make myself sandwiches. The tension fizzed in the air. I slid along keeping close to the walls, listening all the time for footfalls or the uneasy mutter of conversation. Sparks of anxiety flew in through my nose, electrifying the muscles in my stomach, making me twitch all over. I stood behind doors, tense as a cat, trying to work out if the room beyond was empty of menace or not.

In my bedroom, I lay on my back on the carpet by the window, looking at the silver shadows thrown onto the ceiling by a couple of CDs I'd left lying on my bedside table.

I swam through my recollections of you.

I remembered size; size and also colour. Always in comparison to me; like the way you could frame one of my hands, outline it, with one of yours. I loved the rougher tones of your face, your arms, against my paleness. You were all tans and browns and glimmering hairs, and I was all opaque and painted in just one colour.

The *form* of your body was what I desired. It was the solidity of it, the realness. Calves and forearms. Curves and bulges. Planes and angles.

Occasionally, some detail of you would come flickeringly alive in my mind—a thumbnail in sideways movement as you stroked my hand, perhaps, or the vastness of your back, flecked with constellations of delicate moles. Lying there, I flicked slowly, luxuriously, through this catalogue of memories.

The sketchbooks were gone, I remember. Presumably my uncle had torched them or ripped them up. At the time, I paid this fact no attention at all. I existed in a strange, dreamy limbo. I floated above myself, flexing my imagination like a baby kicking foetal limbs while suspended in the womb.

At six o'clock on Monday morning, I was in the bathroom.

I made myself into a different creature, for you.

I'd never prepared myself as carefully for anything. I washed my hair, and conditioned it. I lathered my legs and shaved the little hairs away. I soaked my face with my aunt's cut-price beauty treatments. I cleansed. I toned. I moisturised. I rehydrated. I exfoliated.

I made endless eyes at myself in the mirror. I pouted, to see how that looked. I grinned, to see how that looked. I found the least commonplace of my bras—one made of black silky stuff, flounced with lace—and dabbed it with perfume before I put it on. I ironed my uniform. I washed my stockings and tumble-dried them.

I put make-up on, and wiped it off again. I looked younger without cosmetics.

Coquetry didn't come naturally to me. I learnt the art painstakingly, like a geisha. It's true that I learnt it fast. I had to.

When floating smells and shreds of noise indicated that my aunt and uncle were at last about their breakfast businesses, I slipped out the back door, to school.

The day dragged.

Sitting in Maths class, inflated with impatience, I thought I'd have a heart attack. All my innards simmered in my stomach. My skin was perfectly still, but just beneath it, my nerves all wormed with a terrified excitement.

I stared at the backs of heads, my eyes trying to rip aside all those different textures of hair like a curtain, and reveal you on the other side.

I drew our two ages, yours above mine, in thickly inked figures. Hiding in the margin of my maths book, among a thousand innocent numerals, they did not shout their incompatibility to the world. Still, the rounded 6 of 16, below the acute angles of the 4 in 34, gave me an illicit, sensuous thrill.

Like a general, I waited for battle. I wanted to storm you like a city, surround you, besiege you, until you opened the gates to admit your conqueror.

At recess, you were on playground duty.

I saw you standing in a corner of the quadrangle, sipping coffee.

I came prancing up to you.

'Heya!' I said.

You froze like prey, the mug to your lips. I circled you, smiling. You swivelled to watch me, your eyes quick and worried. I don't think you'd slept much. The skin around your eyes was black with insomnia and worry.

I stood before you, holding myself still, hands clasped demurely behind my back, as though I was singing to an examiner.

'Aren't you talking to me?' I asked.

'Yes, of course I am!'

I danced and jittered before you, filled to bursting with some undeniable life-fluid. The energy running through my limbs was irrepressible. It screamed, *Look at me! Look at me! Look at me!*

'Cool!' I said, dancing a hornpipe, toes pointed.

Your blushes contradicted me. 'It's not cool.' You darted glances at the windows nearest us, seeking spying eyes.

'Is so!'

'Look—' You beckoned uncertainly, retreating rapidly to a corner of the oval. Your jacket flapped out behind you with the force of your strides.

I trotted along at your side. You slowed down. You must have been aware that I had to trot. I rather liked it. It drew attention to my short legs; my littleness.

You'd resolved yourself. You held yourself stiffly. Arms folded, I looked up at you. You were a picture of tweed misery. I was overcome with a sharp desire. I wanted to touch you, to make you want me again.

Firmly, you deposited me on the moral high ground. 'I'm sorry,' you said, shaking the hair out of your eyes distractedly. 'I'm so sorry about what I've done.'

I moved to take your hand, which dangled by your side, in mine. You flinched elaborately away, pretending to wipe something from your palm onto your trousers. I only brushed your knuckles with my fingertips.

An instant expert in this warrior's art, I twisted fear,

stoicism and a big-eyed ingenuousness together and tossed them at you. 'So now—? Don't you want anything to do with me?'

I clasped my hands together before me. I saw your eyes flicker down, registering the way my right hand gripped my left, as though I were, pathetically, trying to hold my own hand.

An outraged sense of decency reddened you. 'It's *wrong*!' you explained wretchedly. 'I've behaved despicably! There's no excuse.'

'Don't you like me?'

That made your limp hands curl inwards. You grasped your thumbs with your fists. Your words came out gravelly, flecked with guilt. 'Yes, I do! That's just the problem, don't you see?' Teacher-mode took over. You raised a hand, hesitated, then placed it resolutely on my shoulder. 'Don't you understand?' you appealed. 'It's just an impossible relationship. I mean … it *isn't* a relationship. It can't be. It's *impossible*!'

I made a Molotov cocktail out of my perceptiveness and lit it under your nose, my head quizzically on one side: 'Are you scared you'd be exploiting me?' I held you in my gaze. 'Because I'm not *that* stupid, that I'd sleep with someone I didn't really want to, *actually*.'

Smiling ruefully, shrugging, you granted me that victory. 'I didn't say that. I didn't mean to underestimate you—'

'Yeah, you did! Look—' and before you could defend yourself, I leant forward, charmingly tippytoed, and planted a kiss on your cheek. 'If you don't want to do anything because you've gone off me, or you're sick of me, or whatever, okay. Fair enough. But don't go all boring and "Oh no! Social taboos!" on me.'

Your admiration of my cleverness, my piercing, unexpected sophistication, was hardly camouflaged at all. 'But what about

...?' you wanted to know, your open hands indicating the green school grounds around us, the brick classrooms on the other side of the oval, the milling dots of distant girls, the sky above.

'Oh, bugger it!' I explained. 'Can I meet you after school?'

You nodded. 'I suppose. Just to talk.'

Without a word, I turned away.

Walking back across the oval, I was already planning the next stage of my campaign.

We had arranged to meed out the back of the supermarket, in the shaded part where they threw the scraps and old boxes.

I arrived before you, even though I'd had to walk. I waited in the darkest corner, next to the blue rubbish skips. Thinking wistfully of my canister of teenage-strawberry-scented spray deodorant at home, I hoped the smell from the garbage wouldn't cling to me and put you off.

For a few silent minutes, I thought you weren't coming. The phrase 'all dressed up and nowhere to go' kept flickering through my mind.

I had my bag slung over one shoulder and my jumper tied around my waist. I'd never tied my jumper around my waist before. Usually I kept the baggy thing on, no matter what the weather. It was extra armour. Today, despite the goosebump breeze, I took it off and sashed myself. Today, my slim arms and the tautness of the tartan dress over my bosom were needed as lures.

I tugged at the jumper to adjust it, wishing there was a mirror around. I thought maybe my hair had got all messy on the walk from school, and tried anxiously to smooth it with my fingers.

Cars came and went at the distant, sunny end of the carpark. I wanted to lean against the wall but that would have made me filthy. I stood up straight, feeling like a china doll on a stand.

Finally I saw your car, driving cautiously (if a car can be cautious) down the rows, as if it was nosing along looking for a park.

The car seemed slightly drunk. It turned a bit too sharply— a genteel lurch—around the corner. The tyres screeched faintly as you stopped. Reaching over, you flicked the passenger door unlocked.

'Hi!' I said, opening the door and flinging my schoolbag casually onto the floor.

'Hello.' You sounded grimly determined.

I kissed you on the cheek as you started the car. 'Where're we going?'

Your hands on the wheel, you answered tersely, 'I'm not sure.'

We sped off.

As you drove, I rubbed the back of your neck, hooking my fingers under drum-tight wads of muscle. My hands looked very slender and elegant, next to the sun-thickened skin that crowded in folds below your hairline.

'Oh...' you said, rotating your stiff neck—'Marry me.'

'Okay.'

You giggled, high and nervous as a girl.

There are parts of my body which are nearly transparent. My palms, my cheeks, the insides of my arms. If you look closely you can see all the blood moving, the veins pumping, the tiny yellow fatty globules gathered together. My fingernails are thin as ricepaper. It distresses me. I feel I'm not decently covered.

But your cheeks felt rough when I touched them. Even when you'd scraped the stubble off, the skin was harder and thicker than mine. I liked that. You were a more solid creature than I was. You were realler.

You kept one hand on my thigh as you drove, only moving it when you needed to change gears. It sounds funny, now, to say that I was jealous of the car. Whenever we had to slow down for traffic lights or pedestrians or a thickening in the traffic, the gearstick took priority over me. My leg, left open to the air by the shift in your attention, thrilled with cold and I awaited your attention impatiently.

Raising one hand, I traced the outline of your jaw. You trembled satisfyingly under my fingertips, your eyes bulging desperately at the road ahead. Both your hands gripped the steering wheel.

'Can we stop?'

You didn't ask me why. Without a word, you turned off the main road and down a suburban side street, halting in front of an anonymous house. With the engine switched off, all motion dead, you still trembled.

'Can I kiss you?' I wanted to know.

'Of course.' You didn't take your eyes off the windscreen.

Stretching my neck, I brushed your cheek daintily with my lips. 'What's wrong?'

'Nothing.'

'I'm making you uncomfortable, aren't I?'

Biting your lip, you shook your head swiftly. I played the false-apology card which, even then, I kept up my sleeve for emergencies. My head on one side, an expression of concern on my face, I said, 'I'm sorry.'

That made you look at me. 'Why are *you* sorry?'

'I don't know ...' I played with a strand of my hair, twisting it uneasily round my finger. 'I've upset you. I didn't mean to.'

You were incredulous. 'You haven't upset me!' Your face was tinged with red. There were tears at the corners of your eyes.

'You're *crying*! I've made you cry.' Silence. 'I'm sorry.'

Looking me in the face at last, you explained, your words crisp and fierce: '*I love you so much it's making me cry.*'

I giggled.

'What?'

'It's funny.' I explained. 'Seeing a grown-up cry.'

That word—*grown-up*—was chosen specially to emphasise the foreignness of your age. 'Over nothing!'

My eyes were wide. I couldn't stop staring. I looked harder and harder, straining my eyes. I tried to tattoo you onto my retinas so that your image would be there every time I closed my eyes.

Squeezing my leg gently, shaking your head, you told me, 'It's not nothing.'

Sincerity widened my eyes. 'I know.'

There was a pause. You picked stray cotton threads from the knee of your trousers.

'How are things ... at home?' you asked, with a social worker's businesslike tact.

I laughed, a short dry burst through my nose. 'Oh, *great*!' I said with rasping sarcasm, thinking of the bottomless silences, the unbridgeable distances, of the weekend past.

Your voice had gravel-flecks of anguish in it. 'Is it?' Your poor wobbling lips couldn't shape the words. Hideous, phantasmal abuses welled up before your eyes. Dark spreading oilstains overwhelmed my bright little life.

''S not much fun,' I admitted, with the POW's shit-happens smile.

Then you kissed me.

You kissed me hard, your tongue stiff between my lips, your hands engulfing my face on either side, fingers spread.

'I won't let anything happen to you!' you declared fiercely, your face an inch from mine. I could see all the ghosts of freckles and the little networks of lines that represented your age. The blood pumped furiously just beneath. Your eyes blazed. You looked at me defiantly, with your chin held high and your eyes wide open, but there was a kind of shakiness to you. You swallowed but did not shift your gaze.

Your expression reminded me of something. I puzzled over this for a brief second, until I recognised it, with a shock of pleasure, as the same rebellious, half-fearful look my friends used to give teachers when they were caught doing something wrong.

'I don't want to be part of the problem,' you told me.

I thought, My God, he thinks I've been abused!

I picked up this misunderstanding, and ran with it. Eyes alight with childish hope, I asked, 'You mean ...' A tremulous stutter, just for effect. 'You mean ... I can come and live with you?'

'No!' You took your hands away from my face, and buried your face in them, comforting yourself.

I feigned embarrassment. 'Sorry!' Sniggering my nasal snigger, I pretended to distance myself. 'No. That's okay. I understand. It's cool.'

Subtext: *I'll just go home to the nameless shadows that prey on me, never you mind.*

I smiled bravely in the face of your distress. 'It's okay.'

'It's not okay! I *can't* let you. But ... I don't want to get you into trouble.'

'I'm sixteen,' I said, drawing myself up to my full, slight sitting-height. 'I can leave if I want. Only if I've got somewhere to go, though! I mean, it'd be worse than home, just living on the streets, wouldn't it?'

This worldly pragmatism melted you. You were a pool of pumping blood and vivid passions, churning at my feet.

'Oh, my darling,' you said. 'Won't you come to my house?'

And I did, remember?

We did it.

We did it in the front room.

We did it in the purpling light of the end of the day.

We did it on the sofa, with the curtains open wide to the world.

I'm sorry to reduce what was, for you, a holy act, to 'we did it'. I should say:

You came to me with anxiety creasing your forehead.

Your hands trembled over my skin.

Your lips quivered as you kissed me.

You were too shy to take my top off. You just coughed and averted your eyes demurely. I had to do it myself.

Neither could you manage my bra-clasp. 'Um,' you told me. 'I can't. Um.'

'*I* manage it. Every night!' The power of my bare chest swept away any sting from my words.

You looked at me with dark eyes full of mingling shame and desire. Your erection seemed to you like overkill, embarrassing over-enthusiasm.

You said, 'Are you sure?'

I devoured you with my eyes. I had you on a plate. I said, 'Of course.'

And *then* we did it.

'Oh!' you said. 'Oh, God!' Your voice was high and pleading, your features hopelessly contorted.

I had another hit of that drug, your face screwing and scrunching and wincing with pleasure so intense it burned you.

Like an opiate, it was addictive. Like an opiate, my tolerance grew with every shot, so that over the ensuing months, I needed bigger and bigger hits to feed my addiction.

Like an addict, I came to live for my drug.

I lay like a thin rag doll beneath you.

Your voice was exhausted. Your words dripped steam and sweat onto my limp cheek. 'Did you come?'

I hadn't. Not even close.

I pleaded virginal ignorance. 'I don't know.'

Your hands burrowed into my armpit, swept along my thigh. 'You didn't sweat. I don't think you did.' You looked concerned. 'God, you'd know, if you did.'

I swear your lower lip trembled, almost imperceptibly.

'It was nice, though.' My voice held just the faintest whiff of look-on-the-bright-side, determined cheerfulness. I knew how to make you insist your love, now.

'Yes, but—' You struggled to explain yourself. 'Every time we do this, I have the most *intense* ... it's spiritual, it's ... the best thing imaginable. But I want you to experience it too, or else it's just ... meaningless.'

Kissing your damp forehead, splaying a comforting hand over one of your buttocks, I suggested, 'Maybe it's just a matter of time. I think it's more complicated for girls. From what I've read.'

'Maybe,' you agreed, hopefully.

'Well now.' You rested your elbows on the arm of the couch and regarded me from between your forearms. 'What are we going to do with you?'

'I'll move in. I'll be your mistress.'

Mistress. The word itself seduced me. Looking at your wide eyes, I willed myself mistress of all I surveyed.

'*Mistress?*' Your voice was half-hysterical with the possibility of it. You winced with the naughtiness it seemed to convey.

My heart caught, fluttering, in my throat.

'Well? Can I stay?' I tried to say it casually, as though you could decide either way and I, fatalistic china doll that I was, would shrug and agree and go my way. But I, too, was struck dizzy with hope. I, too, was winded with the promise of escape.

Breathlessly agog, you reminded me: 'There's *eighteen years* between us!'

I kissed the milky, sweat-glossed skin of your chest, and then let my lips hover there. 'There's half an inch between us.'

'Oh, love.' You sank down onto me, like a wet warm blanket. 'There,' you said. 'Now there's nothing between us, at all.'

*

I stayed the night.

We watched television together, intertwined on the couch like snakes in their basket, waiting for the flute song.

We slept together. Naked.

'I like this,' I said, with the sheets pulled up beneath my pearl of a chin. 'Being naked in bed. It's like being a grown-up.'

Agog at the fact of your own actions, you laughed violently through your nose.

'Like being a—!'

I curled into you, fitting myself to your inside curves. 'It's nice!' I pretended to be offended. 'I *like* it!'

Guttural with emotion, you rasped into my ear, 'I like it too.'

I lay still in your embrace, long after cramps wracked my bent legs, and my folded arms grew stiff and sore.

You slept restlessly. You were dreaming intensely. You wriggled, whispering urgent nonsense aloud.

The next morning, I picked my wrinkled, musty school uniform up from off the bathroom floor, and put it on again.

You went to the bakery for croissants, and came back restless with worry.

'I *can't* give you a lift to school!' you told me.

''S all right,' I said, wiping crumbs from round my mouth. 'I'll walk.'

'You won't get tired? Oh, I'm so sorry!' Leaning over the table, you flicked with your thumb at a large crumb I had purposely left untouched for you to wipe away. 'Messy girl! ... I just ... we can't be seen ... can we?'

'It's okay,' I said. 'Where's my bag?'

'Under the couch. Where you left it.'

You retrieved it for me.

Swinging one leg up onto the table, I unrolled a white sock slowly upwards over my foot. You watched me surreptitiously from behind the pile of breakfast things you were clearing away. Clearing your throat, you seemed about to speak. But, instead, you disappeared into the kitchen, the honey-jar rattling against the plates as your hands shook.

I put my other sock on briskly and without ceremony. Without your watching eyes, there was no need for delicacy.

'Here,' you said, returning with a paper bag in your hands. 'I've made your lunch.'

In the open doorway, you pecked my cheek with your lips.

'Be careful,' you told me. Your fingers were five fiery points burning the skin of my shoulders with the heat of your concern.

I twisted, like a tiptoeing snake, and pressed my open lips against yours. 'I'm always careful,' I said.

Looking back, I saw you wiping at your chin with the back of one hand. Your mouth was still half-open, but whether from surprise or passion, it was impossible to tell.

Passing by my house—my aunt and uncle's house—I let myself in. The smells of the hallway already had a nostalgic quality. Like a song remembered from kindergarten, they were obvious but strange at the same time.

In my room, I loaded up my schoolbag. I grabbed a few bits of underwear, my other school uniforms. There wasn't really much else I needed to take. None of the myriad little china things-for-putting-things-in that I'd acquired had the slightest sentimental value to me. Nor did the fading stuffed frog or his threadbare monkey companion. I'd be relieved to leave the technicolour clutter behind.

I was just about finished packing when I heard a noise downstairs. It was a sharp creak, like the ones our kitchen chairs made when you shifted position.

I froze. My uncle and aunt should both have been at work.

I stretched my ears wide, listening furiously. I wasn't sure if I was listening for a burglar; or because I felt like one myself and didn't fancy a confrontation. But the noise came again, along with a chink of metal on ceramic.

I decided that it must be my aunt or my uncle. A burglar was unlikely to be making himself a cup of tea.

Whoever it was must have heard me come in. The front door was right near the kitchen. It was making me restless, sitting here, straining to be quiet. I just wanted to get back to you.

What the hell, I thought, and zipped up my bag.

As I reached the bottom of the stairs, I saw that the kitchen door was now wide open.

'Hello?' called out a voice suddenly from inside. It was my uncle, but it took me a second or two to recognise his voice; it sounded high-pitched and strained.

I hesitated in the hallway. I couldn't just ignore him. But I was afraid of him, too, as if he were a big dark octopus that might drag me to some murky place away from you.

'Hello?' came that call again, quicker and more tense than he ever sounded.

Making myself as casual as possible, I strolled into the kitchen. 'Hi,' I said.

My uncle was sitting at the kitchen table. He hadn't left for work yet. He had his suit jacket on but it was sort of clumsily pushed up at the elbows.

I stood in the doorway and we looked at each other. He looked sort of crumpled all over, like someone had scrunched him up and thrown him in the bin. His eyes were very slightly red, though he regarded me inscrutably for a long moment.

Neither of us said anything for a while.

'I just came back to get some of my stuff,' I said after a while. My voice sounded uncomfortably small and thin in the space between us.

Again, he paused for a long time, and seemed to be reaching a long way inside himself for a reply. He nodded heavily.

'I was just thinking about you,' he said.

Standing there, unable to run away (I wasn't allowed, it was obvious), my grip tightened on the handles of my bag.

His voice was thick with some potent emotion. 'Thinking about how we used to go down to the beach and you'd always draw a big face in the sand for me with your feet.'

I made a face now. A very slight one, to myself rather than to him. I had no wish to remember being so vulnerable a thing as a child who draws faces in the sand.

He smiled to himself, shaking his head a little.

'Do you remember?' he asked me.

I said nothing. Of course I remembered. Holding his hand and being bought ice-cream with bubble-gum in it which I always forgot was bubble-gum and swallowed and half-choked on. Getting sand all through the car and leaving it to him to clean up.

He asked again, 'Do you remember?'

There was a very heavy question in the air now. He wasn't pleading with me. He was too dignified a man for that. But he was asking me, as strongly as he could, to acknowledge this child, this little blonde girl running around like a fool in the shallows, blowing bubbles underwater with her hands clamped over her eyes for fear of salty water.

'Hmmm?' he prompted, his eyes troubled. 'Down the coast?'

'No,' I said. I couldn't stand the thought. I wanted you. I wanted safe ground, not these sandy dangerous memories. 'I've got to go.'

I turned and left. He didn't call after me as I went. He just sat there at the kitchen table, thinking of another girl.

I loved those days.

I lived them in a silver-filtered daze. An acute daze, a daze of heightened sensations and ecstatic hyper-awarenesses.

All I can think of is the sweep of linen sheets against my skin and the infinite different postures that a man can adopt when he is pretending not to look at something.

I loved the constant, silken touch of your eyes, sweeping endlessly over my yellow hair, and the curve of my belly, and the white arches of my bare feet.

It seemed that I had succeeded in giving myself away. I had foisted responsibility for myself onto someone else. My little-girlness, my thousand-and-one charms, were a sugar-coating which enticed you to swallow me whole.

I flaunted my smallness as other people flaunt bare flesh. I measured my hands against yours, making them slimmer, more delicate; childlike. All my height left my head three inches below your shoulder. All my weight left me light enough for you to carry me easily to bed, when I fell asleep on the couch where we read, where we watched television.

I felt I owned the big hand I held, the big body to which it was attached, the rough cheeks which needed shaving every day, the deep voice. The strength of your desire made you mine.

Orchestrating reactions from you became my overriding concern.

It was all about erections.

You have to understand that my pleasure in our physical contact was, at first, utterly psychological.

Your desire for me was like a physiological weakness, a sort of epilepsy. I needed to see you in its grip more than I needed to eat. But physical desire was quite another thing.

I soon learnt that the faintest indication of arousal on my part drove you into a convulsive frenzy. If I closed my eyes; if I made myself seem spaced-out, abstracted; if my breath came more heavily and louder, I could force you to a fever pitch.

At first, it hurt terribly.

It seems awful to say it now, but I promised you the whole truth, my darling, and you shall have it.

I opened to you, always. But there were times, in those first few weeks, when a dull stinging pain threatened to overwhelm me. All my smiles were grimaces transmogrified.

I think the force of your passion bruised me, too. All those kisses. Your hand always curled over mine. Those soft eyes sliding helplessly, endlessly, over my face. It was too rich a diet, for someone who's lived for years on sketch paper and thin ink.

The truth is that, the third time we had sex, I lay on my back on the green leather sofa, revelling in your face but wishing your penis would *stop*.

*

Separately, we skulked to school and home again. Between one class and another, we met surreptitiously in corridors, sharing quick strained confidences. At lunchtimes, we walked together harmlessly in far corners of the grounds. But only when you didn't have staff meetings.

I could have fobbed the world off with a farce, indefinitely. Fobbing people off with farces is my trade. God forgive me.

But you, precious creature, are too good for those ways. You wore deceit badly. It stuck out on you, like a bright colour. And it grew brighter, all the time.

I remember when Mrs Taylor made my day.

She was the young, cool drama teacher. She liked Mel Gibson and she usually gave us an early mark for lunch. She strode about the school in jeans. Everyone liked her. She was boundlessly enthusiastic and wore her curly hair in high French twists. I can just imagine you in the staff room at recess— before I moved in, when your conscience was bothered by nothing more awful than man's general inhumanity to man— nibbling your sandwiches and listening to her loud laugh and boisterous anecdotes with that shy smile on your face.

Mrs Taylor made my day by saying 'No'.

I was walking at your elbow through the quadrangle. You were telling me, in ponderous tones, about Henry V. I wasn't really listening; just enjoying travelling in your shadow. I liked to watch your hands in their quick gestures, shaping people and events from the air, for my edification.

Mrs Taylor, her arms loaded up with plastic swords and white-fringed royal robes, put her shoulder against the glass panel of the door at the bottom of the Drama Room stairs as we passed.

Instinctively chivalrous, you strode out of your way to

open the door for her.

And from over that armful of props, she eyed you balefully. She refused to pass through the opening you'd made for her. She stood in the doorway while you kept your hand uncertainly on the knob.

'Need a hand?' you offered.

Her white be-ringed hands clasped her bundle a little tighter.

'No!' she snapped. The disapproval in her voice cut into you like ice. Your mouth swung open with the shock of it. Mrs Taylor turned her pretty face away, scowling, and pushed herself through the door.

You cleared your throat, nodding desperately at the doorway.

'Um,' you said, reddening painfully. 'Well. Um.'

Bending like a soldier from the waist, you shut the door, carefully. This was a supremely ridiculous gesture. The weight of the door was designed to swing it shut without help.

You had nowhere else to find refuge from her harshness. You turned to me. You were smiling terribly in your embarrassment.

'Don't worry,' I said. I curled my fingers around yours.

Your smile melted into a look of appeal. Your hand, having nowhere else to go, gripped mine tightly, just for one ecstatic second.

Your nobleness crumbled all away, and you were mine.

I had come to you like a refugee. I had a bag full of pencil sharpeners and be-doodled exercise books, and the clothes I stood up in.

I delighted, in those first few days, to run around the house in nothing but one of your enormous white shirts.

'We'll have to get you something to wear,' you said.

We went shopping in the city.

I tried on everything. You stood, hands in pockets, looking at your shoes, looking at me. The shop assistants thought you were my father. The middle-aged ones cooed over me with you, making you blush. The young ones ignored you.

I clothed myself with infinite care. I'd never really cared what I wore before, so long as it hid me from the world, but now my wardrobe was as important to me as a hook to an angler. It was a vital tool.

I judged the effectiveness of the outfits by the depth of your flush.

It was almost going to be little turtleneck tops and overalls. Just think—I was almost Punky Brewster for you, darling! What a scary thought.

In the end, I settled on short skirts, skimpy T-shirts with tiny hearts on the front, knee-high socks, and little raver sneakers.

'You'll freeze!' you said, when at last you stood on a street corner with the new me.

I let you buy me a sensible new dufflecoat.

'Come on. Put it on.' You grasped it by the lapels, there in the street. Plastic bags full of clothes hung from your wrists, swishing as you leaned forward to settle the shoulders over mine.

I was glad you'd insisted. It really was chilly.

'I look like Paddington Bear in this. Or a spy.'

You did the coat up to the neck. 'At least you'll be a warm spy,' you said.

*

It never occurred to me that you would lose your job.

Honestly.

I came downstairs that first, glorious Saturday after I'd moved in. I had one towel on my head and another round my body. My arms and legs were sleek and wet. I glowed pink.

You sat on the sofa, your long pelican's legs stretched out before you, and hid your face behind the newspaper.

'Hello!' I said, kissing the top of your head.

You were fully clothed. You were wearing *shoes*. Blushing slightly, you answered with non-existent casualness. 'Good morning.'

Sitting down beside you, I nuzzled my head between your arm and your side, and laid it in your lap.

I read the newspaper with you. My eyes skimmed across the words, but I didn't bother to find their sense. I was feeling you breathe. I was worming my hand into your sweaty fist.

You spoke in a sudden burst, like a car not quite catching: 'Look, I've—'

'Am I wetting you?' My arms were soaking your trousers.

'No!' You stared blankly at me. 'No. I've got to leave St Mary's.' The newspaper made a tent over both our faces.

'But aren't you too young to retire?' My naiveté, for once, was real.

'Of course I am!' You tightened your hand around my wrist. 'Of course!'

'I thought you liked being a teacher.'

You shut your eyes against my gaze. You looked as though you had a headache. 'I love being a teacher,' you explained carefully. 'But there are some things that a teacher just can't *do*—'

'Oh.' The possibility that you would chuck me in for professional reasons bore down on me with terrifying suddenness. I felt dizzy. The sounds of the suburb outside seemed to recede, as though I had put my head under the bath water.

'It's only a matter of time.' There was a struggling misery in your voice. 'I mean, for now it's only rumours. They give me dirty looks. But there's bound to be some ... official interest, soon.'

Your leg under my head seemed to be the only solid thing in a vaporous universe. An overwhelming fear of being left alone again, to wander through twisted corridors of my psyche, rose up in me. I felt shivery. I tasted bile.

You shrugged sadly. 'They all *know*.'

A strange lightness flooded all my limbs. 'Okay.' I jumped to my feet. 'That's okay. I'll go.'

And then I stood before you, weeping shamelessly.

They were real tears, believe it or not. I really was distraught. But you see how only the most enormous catastrophes could force me to show you anything honest. And even this display of truth was for reasons of my own. For even then, in the most extreme moment of despair, there was some voice in me, somewhere, monitoring the game of You and I. Threatened with your disappearance, it whispered to me that I had nothing to lose, that I might as well gamble with the truth and see if it worked to my advantage.

It just shows what a strange, alien creature I am! Real tears were worked into the fabric of my deception in a matter of seconds. They were just another tool.

Those sharp tears burnt my cheeks. I thought my chest would burst. I stood there, uselessly, crying loudly like a toddler. I wrung my hands, weaving strange incoherent exhortations in the air.

And all the while I watched you from behind the heat of my hysteria, alert for your reaction.

At first, stunned into silence by my barefaced tantrum, you sat shocked, completely still. The newspaper lay in a sad forgotten heap at your feet. The expression on your face was the same one you wore when watching something appalling, like graphic violence against children on the news—some image abhorrent but mesmerising. You were aghast.

Then, suddenly, you were by my side, your big solid arms restraining my little flailing ones. My body was sunk somewhere in the soft folds of your shirt.

Starkly, you looked down at me. There was panic on your face, as though you'd broken something precious. I kept crying, just to be sure.

'Hey, hey, hey,' you comforted me, speaking too rapidly, contorted with frantic tenderness. I was reminded suddenly of the cat you ran over, and the way you had touched its crushed body—wretchedly, but bound by a duty too powerful to ignore.

You clutched me to you so tightly I could hardly breathe.

'You're not going *anywhere*!' you insisted fiercely into my ear.

I crossed my fingers in superstitious thanks, light-headed with relief.

Guilt made you treat me like an invalid; a sick child. You lay me on the couch and dressed me in the pink pyjamas you'd bought me. You brought a blanket from upstairs and tucked it in around me. You spoon-fed me ice-cream, crooning nonsense songs under your breath.

I was filled with the elation of the narrow escapee; the woman who climbs out of the car wreckage unhurt. My powers over you seemed twice as great for their brush with oblivion.

'Kiss me!' I ordered you extravagantly. Obediently, you bent your head to my lips. I pressed my cold sweet chocolate-flavoured tongue against yours. I felt tears slide out of you and over my forehead.

The next day—Sunday—we went house-hunting.

I stood in a hallway, hands on hips, glancing up the stairs.

I sized the place up. The stairs would be good for clatter-ing hurriedly up and down when I needed to seem madcap. And I liked the overstatedness, the melodrama, of the place. The ceilings were expressively high. The doorways arched meaningfully. There were plenty of dramatic, shadowy places, strange recesses to plunge into. The polished wood shone dully. The darkness of the interiors made my skin look paler—this meant I would draw the eye more easily. The echoes added sig-nificance to every word, every movement.

'This'll do.'

'What?' You blinked in surprise. 'This's the first place we've seen! We've only just walked in!'

The big-haired agent jingled the keys seductively. 'You haven't seen upstairs, yet.' She clipped upwards, heels snapping at the bare floors.

We followed.

Christmas-cake plaster ceilings, slightly peeling. Lumpy paint on white banisters. Wallpaper like a Chinese restaurant; furry designs on satiny backgrounds, in red and gold. The floors were the best thing of all: dark wooden boards, polished till they shone like brown ice. The mahogany and the thick curtains made me think of theatres.

We stood in the centre of the main bedroom.

'It'll be *freezing* in winter,' you hissed.

'Easy to care for,' advised the agent knowingly. 'No shampooing. They don't have to be replaced like carpets.'

I was slapping my sneakered feet against the floor, clunking out a tap-dance. 'They're pretty,' I said. My body was reflected dully, a white smear trapped beneath the varnish. Hands on hips, I peered down at this submerged self. 'I like them.'

'My sister,' confided the agent, 'lives in a place just like this.'

'Does she?' you murmured politely, playing the game.

'Up the road,' the agent insisted, flashing fingernails like red plastic rose petals, as she gestured out the wide window.

'Fuck it!' I insisted. 'The roof works. The floor works. That's all we need.' I wanted the place badly. It was just perfect.

You continued with the standard, ambiguous, house-hunter's patter: 'Well—er—I think we should … I mean, we ought to shop around a bit more.' You glanced doubtfully around. 'It'll need a lot of work.' You ran a hand over the splintered paint that clung to the banister.

'Work?' I said. 'It's fine how it is.'

'It has to be *perfect*!'

'We'll take it,' I said. 'I hate shopping.'

It was more than a week until we could move in, but the spell of the new place hovered over the old one. Your house now felt thin and insubstantial, like faded sixties colour TV.

On the couch, you took me on your knee and nuzzled my shoulder-blades. Now that you'd committed yourself, you wanted praise for your enormous act of generosity.

'Do you like that suburb?' you wanted to know.

'Yeah. The buildings are older.'

'It's nearer to the city, too,' you reminded me.

'Yep.'

'You'll like that. You can go and buy silly clothes every weekend.'

I stretched out my leg in its above-the-knee black sock, pointing the toe provocatively. Under my hip, I felt you go hard in an instant.

'They're not silly,' I said.

You went to school for half an hour on Monday morning, clutching your letter of resignation and the news that I was leaving.

By the time you came back, with a bootful of cardboard boxes, I had already started sweeping your books off the shelf and piling them neatly on the floor.

You couldn't quite believe yourself. There was a kind of reck-lessness on you. It was cute. You were like a schoolgirl under-lining a rude word in the dictionary.

You tried to explain. 'It's one of those defining moments. I mean, when you just throw away everything, because it's incompatible with the one thing you really want.' You made expansive gestures in the air with your long arms. 'I've never *done* anything like this before!'

'I'm glad you haven't made a habit of it,' I replied dryly.
You caught my eye, and barked with laughter.

'I disgust myself,' you wrote in your diary. 'It's perverted. It's
unnatural. Anyone would agree that it's wrong. But, so help
me God, I can't overcome it.'

I never cease to be amazed at the way you castigated yourself about your feelings for me. I know it isn't really the done
thing for a man in his mid-thirties to fancy a schoolgirl. But the
way you beat yourself up about such an innocent, justifiable
passion! When I was a freak, I just lived with it like a handi-
cap; like an affliction.

You made jokes about being a dirty old man, a pervert.

'I should be locked up!' you'd say, or, 'They send people
like me to prison. You know that, don't you?'

I tied my hair in two plaits over my ears, like a little schoolgirl. I skipped into the kitchen, tossing my head to show them
off.

You looked up from the teacups you were wrapping in
newspaper. 'Don't!' you begged. 'They'll put me away!'

Pretending to be offended, I pouted. 'Don't you like them?'

Scrunching the paper away, you came and stood behind me.
Kissing the back of my neck, one hand on my hip, you said,
'Oh, my darling, I like them too much. That's the trouble.'

I turned and kissed you briefly on the mouth. You tasted of
toast, and something else. Cabbage? You hadn't brushed your
teeth yet. 'I could wear a school uniform again,' I teased,
stroking at the hair on your temple.

'Oh, don't!' Laughing, you smiled at me indulgently.

'And white knee socks.'

'Mmmm!'

A gooey smile spread across your face, and you whispered, 'I like you just the way you are, you little, silly ...'

'Oh come on! If you're going to have an affair with a teenage girl—' I took a quick acrid pleasure in declaring my state so plainly to your face, '... you might as well do it *properly*.'

You turned your head on one side, bent forward gently, took my bottom lip between your lips, released it. Holding me round the waist with one arm, round the shoulders with another, you kissed me so delicately that I might have been a bomb that any slightest sudden motion would detonate.

'I *am* doing it properly,' you murmured.

Later, in bed, you reassured me, 'You're welcome to get old, y'know. You can become thirty-five tomorrow, if you like.'

'What do you mean?'

'I mean I don't give a damn how old you are. I'm not a fetishist. I mean, I'm not a paedophile.' You closed your eyes in irritation at your falterings. 'I mean, this is corny, but it's *you*.' Squeezing my hand, you repeated, 'I don't give a damn how old you are.'

But I didn't really approve of that.

I leant half out of bed, reaching for the glass of water you always left for me on my bedside table. I was allowing you to look at the curve of my back and my buttocks. When I turned back, you looked all shy and bashful. I knew that you'd been ogling me. 'It's nice that I'm how I am, though,' I prompted. 'Isn't it?'

'Yes,' you agreed, going red.

That was better.

*

Your awkwardness was like a rare jewel. It refracted your desire into a gorgeous rainbow.

I remember when you came into the bathroom while I was showering.

Flinging open the door, you strode in, targeting the toilet, then—'Oh, I'm sorry!'

I pushed aside the curtain.

I stood before you, sleek and naked, and shouted through the steam, 'What? Why are you sorry?'

Blushing a gentleman's blush, you said, 'I've, um. Walked in ...' In your shirt and tie and suit-trousers, you looked hellishly stiff and uncomfortable.

'Don't be *sorry*, stupid!' I reached two skinny soapy arms out and flung them round your neck, nestling my warm dripping head in your shoulder. And you said nothing about your wet shirt. I *felt* you grin, heard you exhale as you shook your head, saying with your body, *'I can't believe my luck.'*

From the first, you were aware of cliché.

When these tritenesses caught your attention, you did not treat them with the intense scorn natural to children of my generation. You smiled at them indulgently.

On the day we moved into our new house, I cut my foot on a sharp stone on the front path.

I came inside dripping blood, and called you. 'Darling?' God, I loved saying that! 'Have we got band-aids?'

You clattered down the stairs, wiping your dusty hands on your dusty shirt.

'What's happened?' You saw the rusty brown trail across the floor. 'Oh, you're bleeding! Show me!' Lifting me bodily onto the kitchen table, you held the foot in one hand, turning the sole to your face.

You were more dismayed than I. 'Poor darling!'

'Doesn't hurt that much.' As a little girl—five years before—my legs had been all over scratches and bruises. I treated the matter with a child's academic indifference. 'I just need a band-aid or something.'

'Don't move. I'll find the first-aid box.' Rushing back up the stairs, two at a time, you vanished into a series of rustlings. Before I had time to become bored or uncomfortable, you returned, bringing the whole hamper-sized plastic chest with its melodramatic red cross on the lid.

You readied a stack of bandages on the table beside me. 'Does that hurt?' you asked, dabbing disinfectant, peering at my cut with alarm.

'A bit. It's not that bad!'

And then you seemed to see yourself, kneeling on the cold white linoleum, gripping my damaged child's foot with proprietorial tenderness, brandishing the open bottle of Dettol like a weapon. 'Look at me! God, what am I like?'

I shook my head at you. 'You idiot,' I said, for something to say.

'I'll be painting your toenails next, and warning you to keep away from the no-good neighbourhood boys.' You smiled quietly at your own obsession.

I saw that you had outgrown the adolescent need to distance yourself—with sarcasm, bitterness, insincerity—from the embarrassment of sentiment. You did not release my foot when you saw the weakness, the ludicrousness, it revealed in you. Instead, you bent your head, and planted a kiss on the white grubby toes.

*

You went out and bought rugs to cover the floorboards.

While you were gone, I ran from room to room, barefoot. The cold boards smacked against my soles. They made me want to run tiptoe.

Your furniture huddled in the centre of each room. The uncluttered air was sensuous against my skin. I giggled to myself and it echoed. I wished you'd been there to hear it.

I made myself inconsistent, temperamental, coquettish.

When you saw me seducing you, you saw me as see-through, clumsy, infantile. You grinned with love for my baby-ishness, my vulnerability. When I bought lipstick it was far too red. I applied it perfectly, then made nervous kissing faces at you. Laughing, tender tears in your eyes, you melted away completely. I wove this strange false innocence around me, just for you to violate.

It was easy. Little girls have always made fools of doting men, haven't they?

I lived through your need for me.

I could never be so crude as to ask, 'Do you want me?'

No, I had subtler ways and more cunning to make you declare yourself.

The coldness of my behaviours, the manipulation, is only apparent now, in retrospect. At the time, I acted so hard that I seemed to become my own myth. I lived the part so deeply that sometimes, for hours on end, I was able to forget my corrupt self and live wholly in your perception of me. I giggled like a little girl, and managed sometimes to feel a little girl's unself-conscious, extravagant mirth.

I schemed every moment to waken your need for me. All the other businesses of living—the eating, the dressing, the reading of books—were just so much punctuation between the moments when I had you, when you were in my power.

It was as though I had a set of surveyor's equipment in my mind, with dials and knobs all aligned to show the world as you saw it. I'd pose myself, then step back and look at myself through your eyes, squinting carefully as I calculated what you could see and how it must make you feel.

I gave myself to you with relief. Relief, I mean, to be rid of myself, to pass that squalling burden into other hands.

I was a phantom.

I was an exoskeleton whose living, vital inhabitant had departed. My personality was all spread out, as thinly as possible, over the interior surfaces of my body. It was desperate to escape; or at least to pretend to blend with my skin and leave the inside a gaping hollow.

I wanted to be of the exterior, not the interior. I was like some mythical snake which, instead of shedding its skin, might expand to fill a larger one.

'I'm possessed,' you told me. 'I don't know what it is about you, but ...'

I knew what it was about you. I understood that you'd suffered as only a natural idealist can suffer when brought up—*smack!*—against the cold glassy surface of reality. I saw the gentle bookish boy you must have been, made old with tedium, wasted effort, unacknowledged kindnesses. I saw the tired, struggling righteousness of you. You were starving for want of love. You were a delicate, civilised changeling, raised among barbarians and apemen.

I found out all about you, snooping through drawers and opening shoeboxes full of letters. Every day, I added to my database. Your actions and your records were filed away in my mind and carefully cross-referenced.

You'd been married; I think when you were much younger. There was a photograph of her face, and a stack of letters, in a drawer. She had short hair, sprayed stiff, and a thin prim mouth. She'd left you for someone else. You didn't talk about her, except in uncomfortable monosyllables when the course of an anecdote left you no choice. The whole thing stank of betrayal.

Carefully, you reached for details about my life.

'What can you remember about your mother?'

'I know she was scared of cane toads.'

I knew this because my uncle had told me. I couldn't remember anything. My life began when, as a snotty four-year-old, I stood chewing my knuckles in a modern brick church in my aunt's fat arms.

'Are *you* scared of cane toads?'

I'd seen them dotting the sides of roads in Queensland, where drivers had swerved to hit them. In an ancient great-uncle's outside toilet, I'd been startled by a row of them, squatting malevolently along the windowsill. 'They seem ... yucky. All mushy. I wouldn't want to touch one. But I am scared of spiders.'

'Are you?' You had that funny half-smile on your face. You were grieving for my motherlessness.

That sympathy was cheap. It lay close to the surface and

was easy to get. I didn't feel it for myself. You might as well have grieved for my small feet or my need for oxygen. I never knew any other condition.

I am an orphan, but I've never cried to think I have no mother. It all seems like a myth, a beforelife constructed to explain the here-and-now. There was a picture of my parents in the living room at my aunt and uncle's house. It was a big one, framed on the wall. I didn't really like going in there: my parents seemed too much like malign gods who might find ways to punish or betray me.

I said, with false bravery, 'So it's not genetic, then.'

You stroked my hair with the flat of your hand. 'Oh, my darling.'

Toads are unpleasant. Their poisonous backs and dangerous secretions might make you sick. Contact with one might cast a pall over an otherwise pleasant day. Finding one in the bathroom might, in a sensitive mind, render the place unclean.

But spiders—spiders are small and scurrying. They come in through cracks and under doors. They squeeze into unattended nooks and set up business there.

I told you: 'I always used to be scared that I'd wake up and find a spider in my ear. When I was little.' Burrowing in. Finding things out. Reading my mind.

Pulling aside my shirt, kissing my collarbone, you looked up at me with wide sincere eyes, and promised, 'I won't let the spiders get you.'

You'd say, *'I don't know what it is about you, but…'*

But I woke most mornings to find you, slumberous still, pulling me to you, your poor sheet-warmed body desperate, straining for release. I took you willingly. You awoke starving, like a hungry baby that comes nuzzling for milk. You *ate* me, gnawing on my shoulder, leaving red marks that I wore proudly, like amulets or ritual scars.

You would raise yourself on straight arms and come to consciousness through me. Sometimes you drove too hard, your eyes half-drooping still with sleep, the back of your throat rumbling automatic praises of my body. This visceral need, this subconscious desire, was sweet music to me. The pain was nothing at all.

An old friend gave you an office job.

'It's for a furniture company,' you told me. 'I'm going to count sofas for a living.'

'Won't you be bored?' I asked in concern, stroking your hair as you lay on the couch.

'I expect so.'

I made my eyes huge. 'Won't you be sad, not teaching?'

'Probably,' you replied. 'But it's worth it.'

And you smiled at me fondly.

Objects were supremely important to me.

I wasn't just charmingly untidy, for example. I was charmingly untidy with a draftsman's precision. I left dirty socks and half-eaten apples at almost mathematically determined locations.

The way I left my books on the desk could shout volumes about my character, my moods, my preoccupations. Closed and neatly piled for tight-lipped irritation. Open, sprawling, chaotic, for childishness and distractability. Built up into intricate towers for creativity, a complex mind at play.

I was the architect of our surroundings, constantly redesigning, arranging, aligning.

It's taken years of living and eternities of suffering for me to really see the poetry of details, of truly accidental conflagrations of things. To look at your desk here, while pausing from writing this confession, and see: a computer, with a NO SMOKING sticker on the side, though you don't smoke; and the keyboard, with the dark fleck of something immovable, the ghost of sandwiches past, over the 9; and the mouse with its tail all tangled with the cord that connects the keyboard with the screen; and next to these an untidy fan of books, of which the only legible titles are *Little Deaths* and *Concise English Dictionary*—the former being contemporary fiction, new, shiny and smart; the latter being thoroughly degraded with years of flicking, with scribbles on the cover, with the cover half-scraped away in places, with the spine flapping. To see all these bare details parading flat and real before me, and feel a thrill of truth, timelessness, perfection.

Uncontrived details, that is. *I* could never vacate a space and leave a tiny natural shrine to myself, an unconscious work of art, the way you have here in your study. No detail of my life—my body, my face, the way I left objects—ever went unplanned.

I know you loved me because you thought me naive.

I cultivated this. I have never been anything other than an old woman. I've always known more than is good for me.

I invented myself anew. I made myself impetuous, eager, open-mouthed with delight at the simplest things.

Tipsily, I'd take your hand and we'd run down the street to the grocery shop.

You were fitter than me, but I was *young*, and young people are agile and energetic, so I forced myself to run and skip and jump until my heart fluttered and my lungs were like scissors in my chest.

You laughed at my childish exuberance; you in your suit and your tie and your glossy black buckled shoes; your badges of adulthood. I grew drunk on your laughter, on the softness in your eyes.

Taking a gamble, I judged that you'd find scruffiness charming. I was right.

Before I moved in, you were a neat bachelor. You weren't the empty-soup-cans and unwashed-socks kind; not at all. Your books stood in even-backed rows, grouped by subject. Your CDs were stacked in alphabetical order. There was an oft-vacuumed threadbareness to the carpets and a Toilet Duck in the loo.

I left my boots toe-to-toe in doorways for you to stumble over.

I dropped my wet towels on the floor for you to pick up.

My schoolbag lay in the centre of the lounge room, spewing books and chewed pencils and bubble-gum wrappers. I wasn't even going to school—I'd just root through it, pretending to look for pencils, and leave the mess where it was.

I plied you with irregular apologies.

I saw you carrying a stack of my dirty breakfast crockery out to the kitchen. In the evening.

'I'm sorry!' I said at your elbow, as you lowered it into the sink.

'Hmmmm?'

'I keep messing up the house.'

'Oh, don't worry about that.' You squirted washing-up liquid at the submerged plates.

'No—you've been at work till six, and I've been here all day...I feel like I should have been here vacuuming and arranging flowers and all I've done is play Solitaire and pat next-door's cat.' With a finger dipped in water, I wrote *Sorry* on the bench.

'Oh...' You melted. 'I'd rather have you here, playing cards and patting cats, than have a silly tidy house.'

'But I leave my shit *everywhere*. You always have to clean up after me...' Swiftly, I bent my head and kissed your wet soapy wrist.

'And you skip around the place singing, and I go to sleep every night thinking: I am a lucky, lucky man. And I wake up every morning with this little beady eye looking at me, and I think: I'm about to be a lucky, lucky man again.' You laughed through your nose, and tears of sentiment welled up in your eyes. 'I wouldn't change it for the world.'

You did all the housework.

You thought my incompetence was cute.

'I'll do it!' I'd say, wrestling the duster away from you. I'd wipe laconically at the bookshelf. You'd cluck and shake your head and take it from me.

'Here. Leave it to the expert, my darling.' And you'd pat my head, grinning with affection.

*

You bought tins of paint. You bought brushes in bunches. You bought expensive rollers and trays to dip them in.

You stood for hours every day, covering the walls with undercoats and overcoats and final touch-ups. You'd bought new bedlinen, too. Your ancient sheets and duvet cover lay draped over the furniture and covering the floor.

At first, I helped you. I wore an old shirt of yours, rolled up over my wrists. I liked the billowing enormity of it and the way it came down to my knees. I belted it at the waist, like a little dress.

I didn't like the actual work very much. It smelt horrible; suffocatingly chemical. And it absorbed you totally. You responded to my carefully constructed chatter only with token grunts. You watched the brush with fascination and delight. You grinned to yourself, blissful, as the spreading white paint covered the stains and blemishes of age.

'It stinks!' I complained.

Face flecked with white, your old shirt covered in splashes, you grinned at me from the top of the ladder. 'I'm making it pretty for you.'

So you were unmoved by girlish irritability, were you? I changed tack. 'I feel a bit...' I leant against the unpainted portion of the wall, my hand to my forehead '... I think I might faint. The smell's just *really* strong.'

'Poor darling,' you sympathised, without coming down from the ladder. I only had half your attention. The roller in your hand twitched slightly, in eagerness. 'You should go outside and get some air.' Your head bent back over your work, and you painted on with resolute care.

Silently, I went out through the back door. Standing on the steps, facing back in through the doorway, my breathing was ragged with fury.

In the evening, after your work was complete, you strode around the house, shoving open windows and doors. 'We'll suffocate, otherwise,' you said.

'Which one?' You held out two new doorknobs, one in each hand.

'Don't care,' I shrugged. 'They're both okay.'

'I want to make it nice for you.'

Breezes swept through from the back door to the front, rustling the newspaper on the kitchen table, and flipping the pages of my half-read novels.

Passing a toyshop one morning, I saw varicoloured crayons in the window. On impulse, I bought them with the excessive pocket money you'd given me the day before.

When you came home from work, I was sprawled in the centre of the living room, intently colouring in.

'Hello, my darling.' Shedding your briefcase, you dropped to your knees on the floor beside me. Speaking with the slowness and enthusiasm of a kindergarten teacher, you asked me, 'What are you drawing?'

'I'm drawing us.'

It was a picture of a house and a garden path. The two of us, stick-figures whose legs stuck straight out of our round bellies, stood proudly under an orange tree, our stick arms about each other's shoulders. It was drawn in bold babyish strokes. The colours were garish. The leaves of the tree were wide lazy squiggles.

It took me hours.

Dozens of discarded efforts lay shredded in the kitchen bin.

The effect had to be of utter casual sloppiness. It had to look infantile but seem sophisticated, in context.

I had composed myself as carefully as the picture. After aeons of posturing I'd decided that the toddler's bum-in-air position was most suitable. It gave me a slight crampy ache in my hips, but this was as nothing beside the overwhelming cuteness of the way it looked.

'It's modern, so you probably don't understand it,' I said. 'It's about the two-dimensional nature of canvas. And the decline of the feminist polemic.'

'It's lovely, darling. Look, here's the cat from next door.' Shuffling across on your suited knees, you draped yourself over me, planting your hands on either side of my elbows. 'Aren't you clever?' you murmured into my hair, and then, 'Why do you always smell so yummy?'

'Shampoo,' I said, slashing a red, unnatural grin across the face of the cat.

I liked huddling there, in the cubbyhouse of your body.

'The problem with this arrangement,' I pointed out after a while, 'is that I can't kiss you, but you can kiss me. Which isn't fair.'

Answering, you swept my hair aside and kissed me heavily on the back of the neck.

'It's gender inequality!' I protested.

'Bloody feminists.' You knelt up so that I could turn around. I lay down on my back, my face next to the picture. You were fiddling with your belt. 'Look what you've done.'

I grinned. Everything had gone perfectly. Your trousers were round your knees. You'd hobbled yourself. I wriggled my skirt off completely. My legs stretched towards you, smooth and unrestrained. I could run away at any moment.

You took me with relief. Your big body arched and buckled over me. Turning my head as you nuzzled my neck, whispering urgently, 'My baby. I love you. My baby.' I regarded the bright splashes of crayons, retreating like an exploded rainbow across the carpet.

'What are we going to do about your education?' you wanted to know.

The thought hadn't even crossed my mind.

'You need an education,' you insisted. 'You'll never get anywhere without an education.'

I'd forgotten about the future. I was living too deeply in the present; in you.

I shrugged. 'Okay,' I said. 'I don't mind.' At least school would give me something to do during the nine and a half hours a day that you were away, at work.

You enrolled me in an experimental high school a few streets away.

'It's run by an old college friend of mine,' you said. 'We have the same ideas about education.'

Mr Harrison was a big energetic man who wore a cockney barrowman's hat, and illustrated all his words with gestures.

He met us at the front office. His shirt was brightly coloured, stamped with ridiculous patterns. He looked vaguely Jewish. He had a fatter neck than you—sort of a double chin, when he looked down.

He greeted you enthusiastically, wringing your hand, patting you on the back. He smelled of hygienic deodorant lathered over body odour.

'This is my niece,' you told him, looking at the wall behind his head.

Mr Harrison didn't notice your sheepishness. His dark eyes were on me. 'Great! Hi!' He shook my hand firmly, leaving a filmy residue on my palm. I wiped it on my skirt, discreetly. 'I've heard about you.' He watched me keenly, without blinking.

'Hi,' I said, growing uncomfortable. What did he mean, he'd heard about me? What had you admitted to him? Surely he didn't *know*?

'D'you wanna look around?' he asked me, then said, before I could reply, 'I'll show you guys around, okay?'

I must have hesitated, watching you watch him. I must have forgotten to start walking when I noticed how your eyes followed his face, how alert you were to his actions.

Mr Harrison guided me forwards with a heavy hand across my shoulders. 'C'mon,' he said. His breath was toothpasty but also somehow rotten. I couldn't smell anything unpleasant but I held my breath against the stench, just the same. 'Don't want to get left behind.'

His shirt sleeves were heavily ironed. His armpits rustled when he walked.

He showed us around the school grounds, pointing with his olive arm at the oval, the hall, the classrooms. Then we saw the theatre, the sculpture room, the art building.

The two of you nattered on about university, swapping did-you-hear-what-happened-to-*him* stories.

The school seemed interesting. Intriguing people swarmed the corridors, each dressed differently. It was like a tropical aquarium, full of carefully proportioned populations of exotic fish. There was an example of every youth subculture I could think of. There were even some that seemed unclassifiable, like the girl dressed all in pink who roller-skated through the corridor, humming tunelessly to herself.

'No uniforms. They restrict individuality,' Mr Harrison told me, pretending to be serious. 'However, I'm afraid I must insist that you wear shoes.'

'Fine,' I said. 'I've got shoes.'

The two of you laughed indulgently.

You patted me on the head. 'Funny little thing,' you said.

Mr Harrison pulled a Kinder Surprise aeroplane out of his pocket and gave it to me.

As we trotted home, past the parade of funny poky shops that led back to our street, you chattered enthusiastically about Mr Harrison and his experimental school.

'He's great, isn't he? Very energetic. Most enthusiastic man I've ever met. He's very highly educated, too. He speaks Latin.'

My raver shoes were giving me blisters. I was jealous of Harrison and his Latin and the bright smile they brought to your face. 'I'm hungry,' I said.

We were passing a dim and trendy cafe. 'C'mon, then,' you said, and we went inside.

Inside, everything was brown, including the light. Angular artwork hung on the walls.

You bumped your elbow on the doorframe as we entered. The bird-thin waitress fixed her eyes on us. She crossed her arms, impassive.

We sat down.

I fixed my eyes straight on the menu, pouting. I wanted to elicit an apology for your interest in that man, your esteem for him.

You fiddled wretchedly with the forks. That's better, I thought.

You said, 'I'm embarrassing you.'

You *never* embarrassed me, my darling.

Any other man of your age could have had a prosaicness to him—slippers with holes in them, tartan socks, Y-fronts—that might have made me uncomfortable before the blank eyes of a waitress.

Not you.

'What?'

You nodded at the waitress, whispering, 'She looks about your age ...'

If only you understood how deeply I lived through you! My mind was always wrapped around your actions, thoughts, responses. You had replaced my peer group as the standard by which I judged myself. All my dealings with them were conducted on the basis of what *you* would think. I couldn't give a damn what the waitress thought.

'It's okay,' I said. 'It's really fine.'

I no longer ignored my body. Before you, knowing myself bad and believing myself ugly as a matter of course, I'd endured the demeaning, ungainly fact of legs and arms and torso as just another of my private humiliations. But now, I pivoted and pirouetted in front of the mirror whenever I had occasion to go into the bathroom. I took a sweet delight in my twin two-dimensional images: side-on and front-on. I like the swelling of my breasts, and the flat expanse of the belly below, the long smooth hips and buttocks.

The movies often show villains looking themselves coolly

in the eye, but even the mirror never saw what I was thinking. I was just as cute for my reflection as I was for you. I wore my skin at all times like an expensive suit of clothes.

'Oh, you're beautiful,' you'd say.

'No, I'm not.'

This was a strange, inverted lie: my tone was coquettish, daring you to sustain your compliment. But I knew perfectly well, without a second's thought, that of course I was not 'beautiful' in any real sense. I thought of myself as a sort of cold pale slug, inside my skin. I was never beautiful except when your attention made me so.

Your eyes would become wet and luminescent. 'Yes, you are.'

Rejoicing at the strange blindness which had bewitched you, I'd kiss your forehead with my beautiful lips.

Dressing every morning in short skirts and tight tops, I'd make you say your litany over me.

'Do I look all right?' I'd ask, sucking in my stomach and turning my palms towards you in appeal.

'You look gorgeous!' you told me, and the sincerity in your voice made it true.

So I became gorgeous.

I rejoiced in every step I took. I darted along on tiptoe, letting the world run its eyes over me. I knew the air itself worshipped me, because you did.

I thought sometimes, in an obscure way, that you were lucky to have me.

I transformed you. I made you passionate and desperate and blissfully happy and obscenely anxious just by being five minutes late home from school.

I didn't exactly suffer from agonies of conscience. But when I needed to justify my actions to myself, I decided vaguely that my presence allowed you a chance at nobility and grace that might not have otherwise come to your life.

I don't mean that I possessed those qualities myself. I mean it in the sense that religion provides a chance at grace; not because it is real, but because it is believed to be real.

You're a saint, my darling; but even a saint is lost without a god of one sort or another. Equally, if you worship something ardently enough, it might as well be divine. And I was surprised to find how easy it was to create a divinity out of myself.

You rang Mr Harrison up for a date, a few nights before I started school.

You just *did* it, on the spur of the moment.

'He lives alone,' you explained to me as you dialled. 'I thought we might go out to dinner.'

'What about me?' I asked. 'Are you gonna just leave me at home?'

'No!' you said, falsely jovial. You'd been planning just to go with him.

'I'll need a babysitter,' I said. 'I'll get lonely.'

'Oh ...' you said '– the three of us, I mean.'

I was annoyed, but I couldn't afford to show you.

'Fine,' I said. 'Cool.'

I thought that perhaps I could make polite conversation all night, and then give you a guilt-trip for making me hang around with boring old men instead of with cool young people. (You'd expressed promising worry, a few times, about isolating me from my peers.)

You were childishly excited. You changed your tie twice. You thought I didn't notice.

'I haven't spoken to him properly since college,' you told me when you'd made the restaurant booking.

'Haven't you?'

'We were quite good friends, actually.' You were like the school nerd casually—oh, so casually—mentioning that the toughest boy of all is his best mate.

'Were you?'

'You remember…' you asked me cautiously, sucking in your lips, 'he thinks you're my niece?' With your eyes, you begged me to lie for you.

'It's fine,' I said, kissing you on the neck.

You pushed me to a distance, held my eyes.

'It's just,' you said, 'it could be awkward. If…'

I curled my arm in between your coat and your shirt, cuddling into your jacket with you. 'It's all right,' I said.

In the car, you told me, 'He had the room next to the bathroom. It was always flooded. Always! You'd go in and his notes would float past your ankles. He had to wear gumboots to study in.'

I thought that you sounded as though you were quoting an official book of college anecdotes.

'Where are we going?' I asked.

'Piper's. I told you. We've been there before.'

'But it's down the other street.'

'We have to pick him up.'

'Aren't we meeting him there?'

'He doesn't have a car.'

Stupid man, I thought. Doesn't even have a car. But being sulky wasn't part of my game plan for the evening, so I just stroked the knuckles of your hand as it lay on the gearstick.

'Stop that!' you said, groaning. 'I can't go into a restaurant with … *you know*.'

'I didn't *mean* to!' I protested, delighted. 'I was just *patting* you!'

'Sometimes you don't even have to do that!' you confessed. 'I just sit at my desk and remember your *name* and I can't get up to get a coffee or the secretary will see.'

'It's not my fault.' I pouted.

'Of course it's not!' you said paternally. 'It's me.'

And then we pulled up outside a red-brick house, and you tooted the horn.

'Hop into the back,' you told me, as Mr Harrison came jogging up the pathway.

Seething, I did as I was told.

I hated sitting in the back. It was like being a child again, listening to the grown-ups talk about things I'd never heard of.

Harrison made jokes and laughed loudly.

I stared out the window and imagined what we'd do afterwards, in bed.

You told more anecdotes, reminiscing, half-turning towards Harrison. You gestured shallowly with one hand, unconsciously mimicking his mannerism.

As we dipped through a roundabout, a ute beeped angrily at us.

'Careful!' shouted Mr Harrison, and his voice wasn't professional and booming as it usually was. 'Jesus!' He sounded high-pitched and adolescent.

A moment later, he tried to make amends, to recover his public face. 'It was his fault.'

'Crazy idiot,' you said, hardly ruffled at all, and plunged back into your story.

We put on a good show, you and I.

I said, when we got home, that we should take up dancing

and become a famous double-act.

You told me to finish my vegetables. You showed me which cutlery to use, though we'd been here three or four times before.

I asked, cutely, for wine. 'C'mon!' I said, jiggling my glass. 'Just a *taste*?'

'No!' you told me firmly. 'Drink your lemonade.'

But I did think I noticed, once or twice, Mr Harrison watching my face with a kind of alert curiosity.

It didn't faze me. I was beautiful, now. What did one more pair of eyes matter?

Outside the restaurant, as we were leaving, I saw a woman sitting on a bench, snivelling. Her boyfriend sat by her, hunched with discomfort. He was holding her hand but his body was angled away from her.

'I just want to spend more time together,' she said, and her voice trembled. Her cheeks were starred with red. Her eyes were huge, like saucers, trying to suck him inside with the force of her gaze.

He rubbed his lips together distractedly. He didn't want to be there. He was embarrassed. She was flaunting her weakness desperately, displaying the great gaping hole where her innards should be, and begging him to plug it.

Amateur, I thought.

I found that I'd been placed in one of the English classes Mr Harrison taught.

On the first day, I arrived at the classroom early. I didn't know any of the people milling around in the playground.

'So,' said Mr Harrison, fishing in his pockets for plastic trinkets, 'how are you enjoying life with your guardian?'

I said, 'He's my uncle.'

Mr Harrison watched my face for a long moment.

I was sure there was something showing; that the untruth stained me like a piece of food clinging to my cheek. I held his gaze.

'On your mother's side?' he asked politely, lining the little toys up along the desk. 'Or your father's?'

'My mother's,' I said it too fast, too firmly. He must see. He must know. He must.

'Oh, right.' And he tossed me a little gnome, garishly painted. 'Present for your first day,' he said, grinning.

Oh, this catalogue of detachments can't hope to give any inkling of what you are! You are *instinctively human*. This came sometimes as a balm and sometimes as an irritant against my strange alien sensibilities.

I remember us driving down a wide suburban street. We saw a man straining with a leash, dragging a reluctant puppy. The little dog sat, determined, and curled all its legs together underneath itself. The man, fat and surly in a tracksuit, wrenched it, bumping, over the concrete.

'Oh, the poor little thing!' you exclaimed, and your sincerity was childlike. 'The poor little pup!'

It was this intensity of passion, this easy pity, which attracted me to you. 'You poor little thing!' you'd say to me if I stubbed my toe. 'You poor little girl!'

*

122

'You're so *soft*,' you explained. 'Look at this.' You rubbed a fine spray of hair between your fingers, letting it fall strand by strand onto my cheek.

'Horrible colour,' I demurred. 'Stupid, gutless, yellowy-brown. Yuck!'

'No! Lovely sandstone colour.' You ran a finger along the curve of my neck. 'Soft skin. I could sit here and stroke your cheek for *hours*. You *glow in the dark*, my darling.'

'Everyone at school said I must be anaemic.' This was an exaggeration. Rachel had once suggested that I get a tan.

'They were just jealous. Because they weren't as soft.'

Thinking of the hard cruel knot at my centre, I laughed.

'You're beautiful,' you insisted. Poor thing.

Softness is a quality which more properly belongs to you. You loved anything small, anything weak, with your whole soul. I mocked you for it. I basked in it.

I felt like a debauched gentleman of the nineteenth century, who comes back to his home town in a frenzy of remorse and chooses the most chaste and pious maiden to be his bride, hoping that her goodness will somehow be enough for two.

When you told me earnestly that you loved children, I pretended to be offended. 'Why? Who else is there? You're not doing some twelve-year-old on the sly, are you?'

'Don't joke,' you begged. 'I get so guilty sometimes.'

I offered you mechanical comfort, like one throwing a rope to a fugitive wanted for interrogation. I cupped your cheeks with my hands. 'Hey,' I said gently, my soft lips beside your ear. 'If I didn't want you, I'd say.'

'I know, baby.' You did not sound convinced.

'I'm not a baby. I'm very clever.'

'I know, but you're not very old, are you?'

'You don't have to be old to be clever. I know the capital of Laos.'

You humoured me, you shared the joke, but your eyes remained clouded with distant adult sorrows. 'Do you? You *must* be a grown-up, my darling.'

I chewed my lips in dissatisfaction: a little girl who was not being taken seriously. 'Vientiane,' I insisted.

'Is it?'

'And I know the political system.'

'Do you?'

'Yes. It's a communist state.'

'Did you learn that from Mr Harrison?'

'No. I'm just clever. I just know things.' I was a sophisticated child now, speaking your language, but with charming, unjaded conviction. 'I know you're a lovely, lovely man.' I kissed your forehead. 'And if murderers came I'd hide you under the couch and stand in front of it.'

'No, you would not, young lady!' You tickled me gently. 'I'd sit on you, so they'd think you were a throw-pillow.'

I gloried in myself, because you gloried in me.

On the way to school, strangers whispered to each other about my beauty, pointing as I passed. The grass under my feet rejoiced to have me tread on it. At school, the thronging boys and girls saw me and knew that I was the best of them all.

I spoke rarely. I was drunk on the perfection you had made of me. But when I spoke, my classmates were alert for grander things than my opinions of pop music in the playground or

English literature in the classroom. Heads cocked, they were straining to hear the music of the spheres. My gestures conducted the world in its turning.

It was calculated, yes. I choreographed myself. My face never fell into any expression innocently. I knew where every tiny muscle was, every moment. But it was a magnificent, elegant discipline, like ballet.

I'd watch the television, faking absorption, my mouth half-open as though in complete, unconscious preoccupation.

I wasn't listening. I wasn't watching. All my attention was focussed on my peripheral awareness of your eyes. I felt you drink me in, survey my face over and over, the smooth cheeks, the wispy hair, the wide eyes, the expression of earnest concentration.

The intensity of your gaze was like a drug to me.

Occasionally, you'd be overcome. You'd lean in and press your lips fleetingly against my cheekbone, or the top of my head. I counted these kisses as little victories.

'What?' I'd say, turning to you, startled, my smile half-embarrassed. I was adorably uncertain.

'Nothing,' you'd say, and kiss me again.

'*What!*' With my eyes, I accused you of mocking me.

'I think you're wonderful,' you said simply.

In my mind I notched up another few points.

Nestling into the crook of your arm, I'd disconcert you effortlessly.

'Can I give you a blow-job?' was a good one.

I felt you snort with silent, perplexed laughter as you realised the absurdity of your situation. How many men, sitting down to watch mid-evening current affairs programs, find a nubile schoolgirl casually asking if it's okay to suck them off? There were whole Internet sites devoted to this fantasy. There were whole Acts of Parliament designed to stop people who were devoted to this fantasy.

'If you want to.'

'Yep!' I pawed at your fly, trying to gauge where your penis was at. Had I succeeded in giving you an erection yet? I'd lose points if you were still quiescent when I undid your fly.

Usually, however, the thought was enough to send you rock-hard.

Stretching out on my stomach, kicking my legs in the air, I closed my lips around your penis. 'Is that nice?' I'd look up at you, as though concerned by your silence, as though afraid I was doing something wrong.

Head thrown back, eyes closed, you reassured me heartily: 'You have *no idea*.'

The first time it had happened, in our dark bedroom, you couldn't believe I was willing to take your penis in my mouth.

'You don't have to do *that*!' you whispered, solemnly aghast.

I popped my head up, so that you could see my face over your stomach. 'I *want* to.'

Experimenting, I asked, 'Is that nice?'

You made no reply. I said, 'Sorry … I'm sort of making it up as I go along.'

'Come here.' You held out your arms to me.

Feigning ingenuousness, I asked, 'What's wrong? Don't you like it?'

Overcome with my artlessness, my charming frankness,

you stretched loving arms down to me, over the straining bulge at your groin. 'Come here, you dear, sweet, lovely girl.'

With affected concern, I took refuge up by your chest, curling myself round your heart. 'Was that wrong?'

'No!'

I rushed my words, trying to explain. 'It's just I've never done that before! I don't know what to do!'

Stroking my hair, holding my waist, you said, 'Oh, my love.' With an air of the pedagogue who must explain the wickedness of the world to his angelic charge, you said, 'It was lovely, honestly ... the most ... exquisite thing I've ever ... The fact that a little—*goddess* like you would even *consider* doing something like that for *me* ...' A disbelieving shake of the head.

'So it was okay?' I knew perfectly well that it was 'okay'. More than 'okay'.

'Yes. *Yes*! I just ... I'd hate to think that you were doing that because you felt obliged to.'

I raised myself onto one elbow, looking down at you. You were a dusky shadow against the white bedlinen.

'Is that all? You stupid man.' I did my unsophisticated-candour act. 'As if I'd bother doing it, if I didn't want to!'

When we'd expired our lovemaking—when I feigned deep sleep, though only three-quarters groggy—you kissed my insensible cheek with fairylike delicacy, and whispered to the air, 'I love you so much, my darling.'

My darling, I so much loved the look and the sound of you. But I missed the essence completely.

I lived inside a series of tableaux, flickering from moment to all-important moment like an old stopframe animation.

I learned how to keep several realities concurrently true in your mind, and take the best from each as the occasion suggested. Certain things in the picture I made of myself came to be almost completely contradictory, but this, to my delight, only served to strengthen my image in your mind. It gave me depth.

I cultivated a woman-of-the-world attitude at times.

'Of course I'm on the pill, darling, have been since I was fifteen,' I lied matter-of-factly when you asked.

I invented ex-boyfriends. I made up fleeting holiday encounters.

I wove these fabricated men into conversations:

'Oh, I was going out with this guy that...'

'Yeah, I knew a boy who...'

You weren't to know that my previous sexual experience, to date, consisted of one dribble-jawed snog with Melissa Aldiss' older brother at a party three months before I met you. He had freckles and he tasted of sweet coke and sour rum.

You'd nod, when these boys appeared in the conversation, and say with determined evenness, 'Did you? Were you? Oh, okay.'

I invoked the sense of cold, social transaction which characterised these invented adolescent relationships, but it did nothing to destroy your idea of me as essentially naive and virginal.

I woke your jealously with these pin-pricks, and then had the pleasure of soothing it once again.

I'd withdraw my lips from yours, to tell you: 'You're the best kisser I've ever known!'

Embarrassed but proud, you'd dart forward and kiss me again.

And all the time, in your eyes, I was also untutored, completely guileless.

I seemed to know everything, or nothing, depending on the

time of day and the pattern of the conversation and what we were doing.

I could know whatever it suited me to know.

Kisses were the first point of contact, for me. There was no dialogue except the physical. All my speech was just to bring you close. All my listening attitudes were just poses calculated to turn you on. You could have been talking about anything, anything at all. I had nothing to say to you, except with my body.

But now, any lightest token of your affection would seem like the highest blessing to me. To think I've had all of you, safe in the crook of my finger, and I thought nothing of it. To think you've come nuzzling to me, craven, for any morsel of love, and I fed you shreds of plastic. It turns my stomach.

As the spring grew warmer, we embarked on endless picnics.

Behind our new house, there was a little bit of a back garden, enclosed by high walls on all sides. All the walls trapped the drops of rain and shreds of shadow. Towards the edges of the lawn, moss mingled with the grass. In the corners, slime and lichens spread across the bald surface of the earth. Buzzing things hovered there. Strongly perfumed flowers wrestled with each other, day to day.

The very centre of the garden was the only place you could rely on. It was the only place that was safe. The meagre sunlight sucked the water out once a day and made it dry enough to sit on.

We had our picnics there, under the big spreading tree. We

sat on a tartan rug that you'd bought specially. You made me fairy bread and fed me chocolate, square by square.

In Mr Harrison's English class one week, we studied the significance of landscape.

He held up a picture of trees and grass and rocks, all yellow-brown under the relentless sun.

'What does this make you think of?'

'Swaggies.'

'Sheep.'

'Bodies,' I said, and instantly regretted it.

He paused in my direction, and waited till everyone else was looking at me. 'Why's that?'

I fought to keep from going red. I spoke casually, to hide my creeping horror. I didn't want to seem macabre. 'Y'know,' I said. 'Newspaper stories. Girls who go missing along the highway.'

'Oh, right,' he said, his words a little quick. 'The media association. Good.' And laughing through his nose, dismissively, he put the picture face down on the desk. He reached into his pocket for a plastic figurine. 'Have a Kermit the Frog.'

Mr Harrison was a very easy case indeed. At first, as you know, I worried that he might understand the real situation between you and me. He had a way of fixing me in his gaze and asking pointed questions which made me sweat.

But then certain weaknesses of his became glaringly apparent.

He once asked me to fetch some whiteboard markers from his office.

'Top drawer,' he said.

His office was small and cramped and busy. There were letters scattered all over the desk. Photographs of school plays and picnics crowded the walls. Brash trinkets sat jumbled together on a shelf—the source of his endless supply of class-room rewards.

I found the pens immediately, behind some bottles of Voltaren pills.

At home, I asked you, 'What's Voltaren for?'

You answered, 'Pain.'

After that, his loud laugh seemed less instinctive, more forced. His enthusiasm seemed more like obligation, duty. I saw his powerful strides tinged with a kind of stiffness in the joints. Once or twice, I saw him adjust his ridiculous cloth cap to a jauntier angle.

Sometimes, I flirted with the truth. I don't know why.

You told me, 'I was so nervous of you, when I first met you ...'

'I know!' I said. Your forehead creased into lines of inquiry. With an eyebrow, you questioned me.

'I found your diary,' I explained.

'You read my papers?' You were hurt; faintly outraged. 'You read my personal writing?'

That diary was only the half of it. I found everything, in the end.

I nodded. 'Well, how else am I supposed to know what you think?'

An exhalation of dumbfounded amazement broke from between your lips. You shook your head slowly, looking past me at the wall.

'You could just *ask* me.'

Ask you? The idea was ludicrous. What if you were playing

the same sort of convoluted game I was? Or—a more potent fear still—what if all this was some obscure adult game, some grown-ups' affair about which I was too naive to know anything? My mind pulsed with the half-shadowed range of possibilities. Clues like your diary were of vital importance.

With an effort, you conquered your instinctive little-boy, you-looked-at-my-stuff anger. Taking my hand in yours, leaning across the table, appealing, for the sake of communication, of mutual understanding, of your holy, all-encompassing love, you wanted to know: 'Don't you *trust* me?'

I realised then that no, I didn't.

I didn't trust anyone. A hot fear came coursing through me, tingling my nerves and speeding up my heart. What if you found out that I didn't trust you? Would you call me a bitch? Would you understand, suddenly, that I lived in your house, occupied a paramount place in your mind, on false pretences? The idea of you withdrawing yourself, leaving me in a solitude where I could not help but be constantly aware of my own defiled state of mind, was too terrible to bear.

But I was an expert in thinking on my feet. I calculated rapidly, and decided on my next move without the faintest hesitation.

Composing my features into the most apologetic, rueful smile possible, and squeezing your hand with an appropriate urgency, I said, 'Of *course* I trust you.' Looking sheepish, looking shy, pouting a little, as though forced to admit something I found slightly embarrassing, I added, 'I *love* you.'

Fatherly forgiveness won an easy victory over your sense of outrage.

'I know,' you said. Your face creased into a sad, loving smile. 'I love you too, little angel.'

You stood up and came around behind me, keeping my hand in yours, twirling my arm like a dancer. You leant over, enveloping me in your arms, seatbelting me to your body. You buried your face in my hair and inhaled deeply. You covered my neck with kisses. I gripped your hands tightly, as though I were terrified you would ever release your grasp.

I thought, *Phew*! But I didn't stop reading your diary.

My occasional nightmares couldn't give me away. Rather, they were tools I wielded deftly.

I came slowly, *dreadfully*, to awareness.

'Oh, baby, baby, baby. Don't cry.'

I blinked, rubbed my eyes, blearily remembered myself— the existence of my body, my life, my lover. 'What's…?'

We were sitting up in bed, in our moonlight-silvered upstairs room. You leant against the bedhead. I leant against you. A recollection of some keen caustic sorrow was dimly evoked in me, as if by a wafting smell.

'It's all right.' Your arms were smooth around my body, your chest slippery under my cheek.

'What happened? I don't remember.'

Like a Disney father, with scripted, chisel-featured tenderness, you informed me. 'You had a bad dream. You were crying.'

With my fingers I found my tears, a layer of slime between my cheek and your chest. 'Oh! Darling, I'm sorry, I've got you all wet!'

With your fingers you shushed my lips. 'Don't be silly; don't be *sorry*. What were you dreaming about?'

'I can't remember.'

You whispered, 'You can tell me.' I understood in a second

that you loved this, all your compassionate instincts swollen to fill you. I clasped you tightly to me, my lips pursed, rigid, in a kiss frozen against your collarbone.

'It's all right,' you said.

Sometimes, I cried. I didn't know why.

Oh, how hard I used to desire to be like the crowds of people I saw in shopping malls! I wanted so much to be like those who can restrict their tears to appropriate places—funerals and sad movies. My tears used to burst from me at the oddest times.

It disconcerted you.

After breakfast one morning, I followed you into the bedroom. I knelt by your knees as you stood knotting your tie. I leant my head against your calf, tracing the crease of your trouser-leg idly with my forefinger.

Tie tied, you stood back, smiled at me in passing, and sat on the bed, pulling on your shoes.

Abruptly, I found myself choked by violent sobs. They shot from my lips like hacking coughs.

A second saw you knelt by me. 'My darling, my darling, my darling ...!' You tried to cradle me to you, but I was lost in my gushing eyes and tear-dampened hair. A kind of cramp seized my insides. Doubling over, I clutched at my stomach with one hand.

'Angel, what's wrong? What's the matter?'

I could not speak. I heard your panic but had no time for it. I made motions like one vomiting, but I was spewing sobs. It hurt terribly.

It only happened a few times, but it left me exhausted. I'd

sit palely on the bed, catching my breath.

It left you intensely puzzled and worried.

I could always work with it, after the event. I could use those puffy cheeks and lips swollen with blood and darkly shining eyes to my advantage. In fact, those mysterious tears were good for hours of repatriations, inquiries, and soul-searching. For you, I mean.

Anxiety seemed to make you desire me more intensely. You always made the most careful love to me when I'd been crying.

I mixed utterly contrived emotions in with the real ones, just in case.

I made myself seem sad, when it suited me. I remember lying under you, doing my best to look sad and distant. And you above me almost burst with the effort of moderating your passion. It seemed that it was all you could do to keep from slamming into me with the force of your worry.

I kept my face very still, careful not to blink the moisture away from my eyes. The sudden squall which had showered those tears was long gone and I felt nothing except vaguely hungry.

There was always my status as the adolescent girl, who wasn't quite responsible for her actions—not yet—to fall back on. It was an easy act to put on. I did it effortlessly.

I'd gaze out the window, distant, silent.

'What's wrong?'

Tracing the outline of one hand with the index finger of the other. 'Nothing.'

'Rubbish!'

'Oh. I dunno. Sometimes I just get … confused.'

Against the reflective sky in the window, I saw familiar concern falling over your face, deepening wrinkles embedded by long years of sympathy. You said, 'Look … if there's anything …?'

I exercised a trick I'd learned, and stayed silent. If I said nothing, you kept talking, growing more and more emotional as you did so.

'I understand that you're very young.' You shoved your hair impatiently away from your face. Pulling wry expressions, I looked at my hands.

'The last thing I want to do is make you unhappy.'

I nodded.

You said, 'I don't want you staying involved if you'd rather not be.'

Deftly, I made my whole momentary, assumed unhappiness your fault: 'But you'd miss me. You *need* me, now!'

'Oh, darling.' You were an instinctively, compulsively truthful man. 'Yes, I need you, I can't deny …'

'It's okay.'

I'd made you wretched. 'But if you're unhappy, if this is all too much! I'd rather die than think I was responsible for—'

You'd suffered enough. I let you out from under my paw. 'Oh, shut up! Stop being stupid!'

You smiled ruefully, wiping at the corners of your eyes.

Impulsively, girlishly, I threw my arms around your neck and declared into your ear, 'I'm just premenstrual. Ignore it.'

Then I dusted the length of your arms with kisses, and you cried.

*

Things weren't completely perfect, of course. I lived constantly on edge, keyed up with need; supersensitive; stressed. I slept badly.

You didn't mind. You said, 'I love having you next to me. Twitching. Stealing the blanket. Smacking me in the face in your sleep.'

You suffered, like any man your age, from more physical pain than I did. You still had that wry shock of men just past their youth, who can't quite believe that their body really would decide that there are some things it will not tolerate.

Your knees cracked when you shifted position. You got indigestion and muscle cramps and your eyes hurt if you read under too bright a light.

I hated those ailments. To me, they always felt like the worst kind of aggravation—the only obstacle which I couldn't find a way around. Even the best general can't fight Acts of God.

I remember once you stopped right in the middle of things. 'My back hurts.'

It seemed like the thinnest of excuses to me, despite your half-grin of pain. 'Probably from all that painting,' I suggested.

'No.' You moved clumsily off me, falling heavily, face down, onto your pillow. 'Just arthritis.'

I didn't want you to have arthritis. That didn't suit me at all.

'It's okay, isn't it?' I said. Frowning, you felt behind your back.

There was no course available, it seemed, but compassion. I kissed your cheek. 'You shouldn't be doing so much handy-man-stuff,' I told you, softly, sternly—the way you told me to eat properly and dress warmly.

'I enjoy it.'

'It's fine already.' I stroked your backbone with the tips of my fingers. I was dying of impatience, choking with a lust for victory. It was terrible, after so much hard work, to have my prize snatched away. 'There's no need.'

You said nothing. Your eyes were closed.

I waited by your side, infuriated. I was afraid to move, lest my action disturb your spine so badly that it fell completely to pieces.

Another time: 'I can't breathe.' You rolled over, wheezing slightly. I bit the inside of my cheek to stop myself from clucking in annoyance.

'What's wrong, darling?' I asked, laying one hand on your forehead.

'I get asthma.' You put one fist across your chest, breathing carefully. 'Just sometimes.'

I tried to coquette it all away. 'Come on!' I said. I made huge kissing motions in the air.

'I can't,' you told me plainly. 'Sorry, angel.'

I stuck my tongue out at you, making wicked eyes.

You coughed steadily. Phlegm absorbed you. You weren't even looking at me.

'Come on!' I said again. But my voice was lost in the harsh sound of your coughing.

So once again, I was left with no route to follow but the sympathetic one. I drew my hand down over your cheeks.

My sympathy took the form of yours. I suppose that's because your sympathy was the most potent and bewitching that I'd ever known. 'Poor little boy,' I said.

'I'm an old man!' you laughed, slapping my hand away.

*

The world reminded me, once in a while, how little I had in common with the rest of creation. After shopping one morning, I realised exactly what an isolated and unnatural creature I was.

'Raggle-taggle gypsies,' you said, rounding the corner. 'Poor freaks without mortgages.'

We slowed to a standstill behind a red-light queue. I saw from the car window the man playing the ukulele for silver coins, with his trailing dreadlocks knotted Oriental-style on top of his head, an oversize chopstick skewing the arrangement. I saw his moth-eathen poncho decorated with stylised llamas, through which his hands emerged like butterfly wings, afire with obscurely significant rings flashing silver Nordic symbols and purple healing crystals. I saw his filthy bare feet and his bedraggled mongrel dog in its iron-studded collar.

I felt jealous.

You see, his girlfriend, sitting by the patchwork hat laid out to receive coins, tickling the dog under his chin, was dressed in exactly the same style. They were really *together*.

You went on, as the lights changed and the queue began to move, 'The girls at school called them crusties.'

I knew the people that he meant.

'I know,' I said. 'They're sort of aesthetic Luddites.'

With your indulgent, what-a-clever-girl smile, you asked: 'Are they, my darling?'

I slapped your knee, saying (because I knew you'd love it), 'Don't patronise me! I can use a word like Luddite if I want.'

'Course you can, angel.'

I tasted an acidic bitterness as we swished away from the kerbside crusty bivouac. Nosestuds and dreadlocks. Pierced lips. Ankle tattoos of the Chinese character for courage. Eyebrow rings. These seemed such empty gestures of freakishness. They served, I thought, only as identification marks, so that great tribes of the alienated could recognise each other and gather together. At the weekend, second-hand markets in the old primary-school grounds, the vendors of ancient silk dresses and ratty seventies cup-and-saucer sets would instantly all recognise the busker and his girlfriend as fellows. They would share joints and discuss incense and herbal remedies for chronic fatigue syndrome.

I was acutely jealous of their camaraderie. I was born a freak. I lived without hope of fraternity. I carried my perversion with me like a cancer.

'And what are those?' You nodded out my window as we passed the CD shop.

Pressed against the glossy glass, a couple squirmed, kissing. Strait-jacketed by traffic fore and aft, we slowed to a halt.

'Goths, I guess.' I looked more carefully. Under that knee-length cloak of scruffy velvet and the tatty home-dyed lace, familiar features flashed. 'It's Anita,' I said. 'From school.'

Glancing across, you said, 'Oh, so it is. And she seems to have hooked up with Lord Byron.'

The Gothic stick of a boy Anita was kissing wore a flounced pirate shirt and a tight black waistcoat. A slick foppish fringe hung down over his face, obscuring his eyes.

'Although,' you added, 'I don't know that Lord Byron would've had *quite* that many earrings.'

'She was the school freak,' I told you.

'Poor girl. She always seemed a bit misunderstood.'

'Misunderstood?' I said. 'She was persecuted. Everyone thought she was a lesbian!'

'Ah, well. That's the price you pay for looking different, I suppose.'

Oblivious to our nature-documentary, Anita and Lord Byron kissed elaborately on, twisting to some silent music of their own.

She who was persecuted was innocent, after all.

There was a cloistered, claustrophobic air to our house. I cultivated this. It was just you and me. Do you realise that no-one else has ever set foot in this house since we moved in?

I was jealous.

In Religion once, we read this part of the Bible where God says, 'The Lord your God is a jealous God.' Everyone laughed because Rachel McCormac said, 'So he means, like, don't be a Buddhist.' And the teacher explained how God extended this to mean he was jealous of, not just other gods, but any image at all, except his. And that's why we're not supposed to make graven images (even though we do) and why Muslim art is geometric and doesn't represent anything real.

I was jealous like that, like God.

I couldn't bear you to have friends. You spoke, occasionally, to your brother on the telephone. My stomach used to twist in on itself, gushing acid, if you laughed during these conversations. I hated you, briefly, while you swapped anecdotes and inquired after your mother.

I used to pretend to be all courteous and adult. I'd make a show of respecting your privacy, leaving the room as soon as you picked up the phone. But I listened to every word, pressed against the wall outside the door.

*

You loved buying me things.

You'd come home from work with a book, giftwrapped and be-ribboned: 'I thought you might like this.' You brought me expensive boxes of chocolates: 'Have you tried these? They're delicious.' You offered up exotic cakes and CDs like gifts to a benevolent idol.

I really wasn't used to this much material attention.

'I'm home!' you'd call. 'I've bought you some new socks.'

'Is that a hint? Are you sick of me stealing yours?'

'No. I just like to get you presents, that's all.'

Any service you could perform for me you seemed to count as a privilege.

I came home through the late afternoon from Art class. I swung the door open on darkness and chamber music.

You were in the lounge room with a bottle of champagne and a box of expensive liqueur chocolates. As soon as I entered, you jumped up and helped me off with my coat.

'Candles!' I crowed.

'D'you like it? I've made dinner, too.'

Stretching up on tiptoe, I kissed you on the cheek. One perfect rivulet of golden hair wisped by my eye and down my cheek. You stroked it back behind my ear. That's what it was there for. 'Can I have a drink?'

'Sit down.'

I did.

'I shouldn't really give you alcohol.' Your eyes were twinkling; your mouth pursed sheepishly.

I yawned expansively, noisily. Grinning, you poured me the drink. As I reached up to take it, you snagged your foot under the rug and lost your balance.

Sudden cold streams of champagne ran down my legs, under my thighs, and collected on the couch in a sticky pool.

'Oh!' You sounded heartbroken. Standing like a pantomime character, with the upraised bottle still in your outstretched hand, you wailed, 'It wasn't meant to be like this!'

But you were wrong. It couldn't have been more perfect. Standing crooked with your own clumsiness, you belonged to me more than ever.

'It's all right,' I said, kissing you, bestowing forgiveness like a knighthood, the gift of a gracious monarch. 'I still love you.'

Here is a snapshot of perfection.

I had gone upstairs for a book I'd left by the bed. It was Saturday morning. It was sunny. I went over to the window, opened it, felt the new-minted air on my cheeks, looked down on the green garden below. I let my eyes drift, unfocussed, over the great divine mass of leaves and lawn.

Silently you followed me up the stairs; silently you stood in the doorway, watching me.

And then I felt your kiss on the back of my neck. You encircled my waist with your arms, hands butterflied on my belly, drew me into you. I melted against your chest, catlike rubbed my head at your chin. All my instincts whispered, *Take me take me take me.*

I turned at last in your arms.

You said, 'I want you.'

You were driving out the demons with every thrust.

*

Afterwards, we lay together.

'Vulnerable,' you said, not moving.

'What?'

'Men. At this point in the, er, proceedings ...'

Kissing the top of your head, arching my stomach to feel yours, gliding my hand over the vastness of your warm damp back, I said, 'Don't worry. I'll look after you.'

'Oh, my princess, you've already done that!'

'Mmmmm.'

I can't possibly write down the sound.

You know the one I mean.

I came downstairs after my shower, dressed in your pyjamas—to emphasise my shortness and the slenderness of my waist—and found you lying on the couch. I knelt in front of you, and kissed you on the mouth. Without a word, as though responding to a deep, infantile need, I unbuttoned the pyjama top, guiding your mouth maternally onto a nipple, stroking your hair as you suckled.

And you'd go: 'Mmmmm.'

It was a higher-pitched, more feminine tone than your usual, bass voice. It was you admitting that you needed me. Ten points.

I can't tell you how satisfying I found the sight of your big legs, curled on the cushion. I loved to see your chest swivelled towards me, your arms lying limp and forgotten by your sides. I loved to see your whole body in that mute C-shape, every shred of your attention centred on the point of contact with me. You eyes closed, your face contorted, you suckled urgently.

'Mmmmm.'

I'd sell my soul to hear it now.

*

Sneakily, I drew you.

I drew you as I saw you from the upstairs bathroom window, outside in the garden with your jeans rolled up and a watering can in one hand. I drew you cooking. I drew you reading the newspaper. I drew your face from a thousand aspects.

You'd find my scraps of sketches about the place, when I was called away, and left my interrupted work where it lay.

'They're very good,' you'd tell me. 'You're very talented, angel.' With that little pout of self-deprecation. 'Except for your choice of subject matter. Why don't you draw some young Adonis with his shirt off?'

I knew what to do when that happened. I saw the pinhole and plugged it with my whole body. I slid the flap of paper from your hands, tossing it, extravagantly forgotten, onto the floor. I flung my arms around your neck, pulled your face downwards with all my strength, kissed you with all the passion I could muster. 'I don't want a stupid Adonis!' I whispered fiercely. (I would have liked to stamp my foot, to add to the unselfconscious childishness of my agitation, but your height left me on tiptoe.) 'I want *you*.'

You looked at me looking up at you. My mouth was open, as though straining to say more but unable to find the words. It was an expression which came easily to me when I needed to mask inarticulateness. With delicate fingers, you smoothed back my hair, which was damp and did not need to be smoothed back. My eyes were wide with innocent passion.

'Oh, I want you too.' Your eyes were moist with sentiment. 'I want to do everything for you. I want to love you so hard.' Gathering me in your arms, whispering ticklishly into my ear, you added, 'Sometimes it scares me, how much I need you.'

I thought that was a bit tacky but I didn't say anything.

The drawings don't stir me, now. You could be anyone. I'm used to seeing you from an inch away. I remember the side of your nose as I kissed you. I remember your eyes closed and your face very still, kissing me. I remember your eyes growing big with worry too, and the backs of your hands that I stroked, and your square fingers that touched my face. You're all made of moving fragments. The man in the pictures is still and whole, like a butterfly under glass.

Our little jokes were devices only. Our easy humour was a gimmick to keep you close.

Now, without you, they really do seem funny.

Watching a lifestyle program, I said, 'Maybe I'll go to South America.'

'Would you like to go there?' Already calculating airline tickets, passports, customs, time off work, time off school.

'I could buy a small country and start a tin-pot dictatorship. I'd have a General called Enrico and I'd pay my mercenary army in drug money.'

'Could I come? I could write propaganda for you.' You were being shy.

'No,' I said, blithely refusing to let you play. 'I'd write my own propaganda, and draw my own posters. I'd live in a hacienda and spend my time founding a dynasty so I could assassinate them one by one.'

'Can't I come? I could wave you with a palm-leaf and keep you cool.'

I shook my head. 'No. Your name's not Chico.'

'I could change it. *Your* name's not…' You couldn't think of an appropriate name.

'But I won't need my name,' I explained patiently. 'I'll go by *El* something. El Commandore.'

Every so often, I reminded you of my ethereality.

I took you to places swarming with young people. I pretended to feel at home among those tribes of aliens.

I wanted you to see me as one of them, like a bee which might at any moment return to the swarm. I made it clear that I was as hard to pin down as a ray of moonlight, as unstable as a soap bubble. I wanted to wake in you the suspicion I might flitter on and disappear at any moment.

We rode the bus to the markets one Sunday. It was hot. Our legs stuck to the seat. My legs stuck to your legs. We had to peel ourselves loose.

I jumped from the bottom step of the bus onto the kerb, and led you to the great wire gates.

Socialists with shaved heads tried to press left-wing newspapers into your hands. Awkwardly, you folded your arms.

'Bizarre,' you murmured. Or maybe it was 'Bazaar.'

You were startled by a giant koala seeking donations.

'Stop the woodchipping?' it asked, shaking its bucket imperiously.

'Um,' you said, plunging your hand into your pocket. 'Oh, er.'

And you gave it two dollars.

I led you past the portals and into that strange carnival.

The place was thronged. Fiddle notes thrilled the air.

Turning to see that you were still behind me, I saw chimes swing sweetly about your head. You ducked, grinning apologetically at the woman who kept the stall, and trotted after me.

I knew it was a risk. There were fifteen-year-old girls *everywhere*, clumped in slow-moving, giggling troupes. They wore midriff tops and had pierced bellies. They slung rough hessian bags across their lithe bodies. Their hair was henna'd red; dyed green; or shaved completely away. They pawed sensuously over silver medallions and they held empty sea-green bottles up to the light. They laughed loudly, and tickled each other. They were charming and unaffected.

It was a test of your faith.

I wove through the crowds like a rabbit. You, lumbering bloodhound, became the inefficient hunter. Spying a trinket, I'd loosen my hand from yours and duck into a space between two fat women that I knew was too narrow for you.

When you caught up with me, moistening your lips with a hesitant tongue, I'd turn shining eyes up at you. Holding up some ring or chain or beaded bracelet, I'd say, 'Isn't it *gorgeous*?'

And you'd buy it for me.

I remember the time I made you take the day off work, just to hold me.

I used my trembling voice, my uncertainty, like catnip.

I'd woken before you. Our faces were inches apart. You slept on your stomach, one fist nestling next to your mouth. With your rounded nose and half-open mouth, you could have been a three-year-old.

I smiled at you, tenderly.

I wanted you awake. I wanted you to see me smiling, tenderly.

Gently, I blew on your forehead. Flinching, you stirred. I blew again, harder. Half-mumbling, you rolled onto your side.

'Hello!' I chirped, cupping your cheek with one hand.

You smiled. 'I love waking up,' you told me, 'and seeing that bright little eye staring back at me.'

Because I could, I reached under the covers, taking your erection in one hand.

'Don't go to work.' I pulled, very gently, to watch you close your eyes and wince with pleasure.

'I have to go to work.'

Moving my hand up to the smooth skin of your shoulder, I slithered myself in close, breathing warmly on your forehead. 'No, you don't.'

Savouring my presence, smiling blissfully, you said, 'Mmmm ... yes, I do.'

Taking my hand back, leaving a sudden cold, exposed spot on your shoulder, I put on my best protruding lower-lip pout.

'I'll be home again soon,' you promised.

I shook my hair over my eyes. With one hand, you smoothed it away. 'I could come home for lunch.'

Silently, I shook my head.

'I could try and get off early. I could say I had a dentist's appointment.'

'Call in sick.' I kissed your cheek, delicately.

'I can't, baby. I've got to work. And you've got to go to school.'

'I feel sick.'

Concern massed in your eyes. 'Sick? What's wrong?'

I laid my arm over my face, curling one hand over my ear,

and peeped at you from under my wrist. 'Love sick.'

It was tacky, I admit; but it worked, didn't it?

'Oh, my angel.' You melted. I watched with satisfaction as your resolve all dissolved away, like a disprin in water.

'I just want to feel myself next to you,' I confided, still hiding behind my arm. 'I just want you to lie on top of me and keep me from *flying away*.'

Wriggling downwards, you brought your eyes level with mine. 'I think,' you told me sincerely, 'that if I did that, we'd both just shoot up into the air.'

I moved like lightning, flinging my skinny arms around your neck and pulling myself in close. 'We'd float out the window.'

'We'd waft away on the breeze.'

I used your cheek as a pillow, rubbing gently at the night's stubble growth. 'Will you stay with me today?'

You turned under me, onto your back, your arms under my arms, your hands along my shoulder-blades, your wrists pressing against my waist.

'Of course,' you said.

My days at school passed in a dream.

I mean, I talked to people. Sue, the most popular and most pleasant girl in Year Ten, took me under her wing. She insisted I sit with her friends at lunch, and made a point of asking my opinion every so often. She had dimples and a wide smile. I hardly saw her.

I talked, I ate my lunch, I did my schoolwork, but I did all these things on autopilot. When I walked, I carried a low, heavy cloud over me. A heatwave. It made me squint as I walked. At my desk, I thought of your limbs and liquids, my eyes half-closed in a somnolent daydream. Looking out of the window at the trees, I was taking your fingers in my mouth. Walking down the lino-swathed corridor, I was not listening to my peers shout, whisper, laugh, gossip.

I was saying: 'I want you to ...'

I was listening to you say: 'I want you to ...'

I was glutted with you.

I was greedy for more.

At night, you read to me. You liked classic children's stories. We got through all of *Alice in Wonderland, Through the Looking Glass*, and most of a book of Hans Christian Andersen fairy tales. You got quite into them. It was cute.

I chose the books. It was easy to react to them—little eyes wide open, eager, distracted, absorbed. I'd lie curled with my head on your knee; or you'd sit up in bed and I'd lean against you, looking up. For variation, I could put the tip of my thumb against my front teeth as though I'd been about to suck my thumb but had become so enthralled by the story that I'd left it there. Or I could pretend to fall asleep in uncomfortable positions, like a cat.

This took patience and endurance. My body would scream with cramps while you ever-so-cautiously discovered that I was asleep—calling my name and stroking my hair gently.

But it was a useful investment. Invariably, the next day, you'd say, 'You fell asleep with your legs all twisted together and one arm behind your back, last night.'

Then I could say nonchalantly, 'Did I?' and you could nod and say approvingly, 'You must be made of rubber!' I must be young and pliant, was what you meant. One point to me, despite the kink in my neck.

There were certain minor rewards during the stories, too. I liked the passing smiles you threw me. I liked the way you leant in, dramatically, at the most exciting moments, your voice exaggeratedly clear, the way one speaks to babies.

But I hated the sound of your voice. At least, I hated to hear it so monotonously pronounce words that had nothing to do with *me*. Those unexpected, unwanted sentences disturbed the surface of my consciousness.

I was always trying to think about you. Eyes closed or glazed, I'd be imagining kisses, grasping hands. Endlessly, I'd drift into daydreams in which I stood on tiptoe, moulding my body to yours, letting you give me a shape. (All my daydreams then were small-scale but engulfingly intense. I'd spend hours devising a single kiss, a single movement of your hips.)

Your voice nattering on about the Mad Hatter and the Queen of Hearts was an annoying noise which kept me from important dreams.

My desire for you is difficult to quantify. At the beginning, it was not so much the *act* of sex as the *idea* of it; not so much the heavings of physiology as the compulsions of psychology.

At the beginning, all my sexual responses were artifice. I gasped when I could just as easily have remained silent. My curiosity alone was as instinctive and severe as your desire.

I remember the first moment when the possibility of physical arousal woke in me.

You didn't notice anything different. I didn't let you.

It happened after school one evening.

We were on the floor of the lounge room, in front of the heater.

I lay on my back with my hands behind my head, sucked in my stomach, and let you touch me.

You lay on your side, propped on one elbow. Softly, you ran your hands all over my body.

What I remember most is your eyes, half-lidded. You were somnolent with it, engorged all over, blood flowing just below the surface of your skin.

I had my eyes closed. I became so drugged, so dreamy, so relaxed, that your gentle touch on my belly, your light fingers running over the curve of my hips, actually provoked an involuntary reaction from me. I twitched suddenly, victim of a swift, unplanned contraction of the abdominal muscles.

You smiled. 'Is that nice?'

I nodded, as I would have nodded had you tickled me, had your hands been slightly too rough, had your caresses awoken a latent itchiness in my skin.

'Yes!' I affirmed, with my usual enthusiasm.

And you smiled with quiet pride, as you always did when I said you were arousing me.

I thought, So this is what all the fuss is about. Normal people must feel like this everytime!

More and more often, I was called from my dreaming by Mr Harrison. He was very subtle. When I was staring out the window, he'd cross the classroom, and fiddle with the blinds, without pausing for breath. He'd insert himself between my eyes and the blank blackboard I was using as a backdrop for my thoughts, whistling tunelessly so I couldn't concentrate. He'd ask me a question, oh so casually, and I'd have to fumble quickly around in my forebrain and find the answer.

Waiting for my answer, he'd regard me with a sharpness, an alertness, that I found discomforting.

I didn't care if he knew about us; not exactly. I wasn't afraid. Just slightly uneasy. I saw the way my jumpiness made you jumpy. You took to standing behind me as I sat reading, massaging my shoulders.

I screwed them up. I made them tense.

'Okay?' you asked.

'What?' I said, distracted.

'Everything okay?'

'Fine.' On the spur of the moment, fine didn't mean fine at all. It meant stressed as hell. I was exploiting an important insight: the genuinely young and immature all have a burning desire to be thought of as grown up, to think of themselves as mature.

'Tell me, baby.'

I made as if to read my book. 'Nothing.'

'It's not nothing.' You stood awkwardly, obliged by your worry.

Thinking rapidly, I discounted the idea of pouting babyishly, and instead turned to face you for the moment of my declaration. 'It's Mr Harrison,' I said.

My line was soap-opera perfect: sharp, clear, dramatically delivered. Your puzzlement was exactly the right reaction, too.

'What?'

'He knows!' I said, underscoring the intensity, the seriousness of the situation with the crispness of my concerns. The book lay forgotten on my lap.

'He doesn't know.'

'He gives me funny looks.'

'You're imagining it.'

'He's always *asking* me things. He *watches* me.' I said it almost pleadingly, at last allowing the vulnerable little girl beneath the grown-up act to show through. It was a master stroke.

'Oh, baby,' you said. I just kept looking up at you with this uncertain expression on my face, as though to say, Tell me, tell me, I don't understand.

I decided to stand up. I let you fold me into your arms.

'Oh, my darling.'

'What?' I allowed the sound of imminent tears to appear in my voice. I let my little body go rigid, quivering, in your embrace.

'I told him about your parents.'

I pulled away. 'What's *that* got to do with it?'

'I shouldn't really ...' you demurred.

Scenting a secret, I instigated procedures to find it out. 'What?'

'I shouldn't say.'

I wasn't going to let you stand there with that look of abstract importance on your face while I floundered about in ignorance. 'You can't not *say*! Not when it's this important! It isn't fair!' Hands on hips, I stamped my foot.

'Hey, hey, hey,' you soothed me, worriedly. 'It's nothing bad. It's nothing bad about you.'

'I've been so worried!' I insisted, gratified.

You took a deep breath. The look on your face was familiar—the tension of having to explain to a sheltered child about something terrible. I was on safe ground now.

'*What?*'

'He killed his sister,' you said simply.

That surprised me. 'What?'

'He didn't *kill* her. He was driving and they had an accident. She wasn't wearing a seatbelt. It was ages ago.'

I thought, Ho-hum. So now he's got a weird thing about the children of car accidents. Simple.

I was very careful not to let this matter-of-fact emotion show in my reply. 'So...you mean, he feels responsible for me?' I said, wonderingly. 'Because he was in a car crash?'

'He feels responsible for a lot of things, I think.'

'He doesn't seem like someone with a terrible burden.'

'No. He used to joke about it. He'd apologise to us—we had to drive him everywhere. Someone would say, "I think we're gonna be late." And he'd say, "Better late than dead on time." Just stupid things like that. And we'd all laugh.' Your eyes were troubled.

I moved to shift the focus of your sympathy back onto me, where it belonged. 'I'd really rather'—my voice was the model of emotion mastered by a huge effort of will—'you didn't say anything. To people. About... *you know.*'

'Oh, darling—!' I'd struck a rich vein of guilt.

Quickly, I added false courage to my act. 'It's all right!' I insisted, my lips twitching, belying the vulnerability beneath my bravery. 'It's just a bit... y'know. I'm a bit sensitive about it. But then it seems wrong, doesn't it, to ask people for extra sympathy because of...? So I'd rather they just didn't know.'

My denial of any need for extra sympathy had exactly the opposite effect on you. I knew it would. You pulled me tightly to you, your fingers splayed across my shoulder-blades.

*

After that, Mr Harrison's history was obvious in every step he took. I watched him parading ridiculously around, locked within his own private Santa act, working every moment, arranging shelter for the boy whose parents kicked him out of home and introducing a remedial maths course and attending the endless mediocre school drama productions, clapping loudly after every scene.

I could smell it. I could taste it on my tongue.

It was interesting to watch; but, to me, slightly ludicrous, faintly appalling. Imagine allowing just anyone to see inside you, to see how you worked. He was like one of those toys where you can see the clockwork, and you know how every last cog turns.

I couldn't believe how close to the surface you adults wore your griefs. If I could hear echoes of this death in his every word, what must his secretary see?

I knew you had a secret too.

I was watching you every minute.

Even as I pranced around, pretending to be a carousel horse, singing to myself at the top of my uninhibited voice, I was monitoring you with all my peripheral senses. I was waiting for the incomparable sensation of those green eyes burning into me, seeking solace, seeking comfort.

We had been playing Trivial Pursuit on the living room floor. You were letting me win—hinting outrageously, and giving me three guesses at every question. I lay with my chin on my forearms. My bare feet dug around at the edge of the rug. My toes played with the fringe.

'How did Marie Curie die?' You sat rather stiffly on the

floor, your back against the sofa.

I knew the answer perfectly well. I pursed my lips and pretended to be figuring things out with slow movements of my lips. 'She ... blew herself up with an atom bomb.'

'No, my darling. Think about ... nuclear accidents.'

'Stop hinting! She—she she she—was getting up one morning when she slipped on a banana skin and fell over and impaled herself on a Geiger counter.'

'Very, very close. Think about Chernobyl.'

'*Bipp ... bipp ... bipp, bipp, bippbippbippbipp ...*' I imitated the Geiger counter with my hand too, tickling you under the arm. Your cheeks grew round and coy as you giggled, slapping at my hand.

'Stop that! How did Marie Curie die?'

'I dunno. Radiation poisoning? Leukemia?'

'Clever baby! A piece of pie for you!'

The telephone rang.

You reached easily across to the little low table on which it sat, and fished up the receiver.

'Hello?'

Your attention was irrevocably elsewhere. I laid my head on your thigh.

'No.'

With my cheek, I felt your leg tense.

I lay and strained myself, listening, alert for any clue.

'No,' you said again, and hung up.

You acted normal, but there was an edge to you, a distance, that drove me mad.

A few nights later, as you climbed into bed next to me, I

awoke from a feigned sleep, and took my thumb out of my mouth.

Sucking my thumb was my new gimmick. I'd been planning it carefully while you sat watching a French film downstairs: how you would enter the room, tiptoeing heavily, trying not to wake me. How you'd see me curled into a ball, thumb in mouth, and smile at my sleeping form. How I'd awaken gradually, stretching. How I'd look at my thumb, embarrassed to be caught in so flagrant an act of babydom. How you'd be charmed.

Childishly, I rubbed at my eyes with the backs of my hands.

But some beast outside was spoiling my performance. A dull caterwauling drifted up into our bedroom from the street below.

You sat, frozen, head cocked, listening intently.

I yawned expansively. 'Hey, baby,' I said, sitting up a bit, so that you could see my breasts. The sight of my perfect, unashamed nakedness often stirred you to a display of affection. I held my shoulders back carefully.

You smiled at me, but you were distracted.

Somewhere outside, footsteps shuffled along concrete. They were too obscure and monotonous to locate. Your eyes darted this way and that, like goldfish in bowls. You weren't looking at me. Your attention was elsewhere. Some passing party guest was ruining my show.

Suddenly, you started violently. From outside came the sound of glass shattering, and a river of guttural, undefinable oaths.

'It's just someone going home from the pub,' I said.

'Mmmm.' You were hardly listening to me, all your attention concentrated on the darkness outside the window. In the lamplight, you were agleam with tension, like a deer that's caught the scent of dogs.

There was a shuffling and a scuffling, but they were quieter now.

'Or some drunk old man.'

You nodded briefly, still listening. The strange noises receded into the night.

'I'm going back to sleep,' I announced, lamely.

'Mmmm,' you said again.

I really did drift off. I was very tired.

Uncertain hours later, I woke fleetingly in the night. You were lying stiff as metal, eyes wide open. You didn't try to touch me with an extended hand or leg. You didn't press your flank against mine as you usually did, keeping alive our contact even through our separate sleeps.

You were thinking of something else.

On my way to school next morning, I saw shards of green glass catch the sun like ragged emeralds scattered along the side of the path.

All day, I burned with curiosity and wild jealousy. I couldn't bear you to have this retreat, into your preoccupation. I needed all your attention.

That evening, I jumped the side wall and let myself in through the back door, as usual.

It was obvious in an instant that something was badly wrong.

In the lounge room, you were sitting on the floor, your back against the couch, long legs flung out before you anyhow.

Your suit was rumpled. One trouser-leg had ridden up almost to the knee. Your leg between the sock and the suit looked skinny and juvenile.

You weren't exactly crying. You had one knuckle in your mouth though, and your eyes darted with terror.

There was a scratching knock on the front door. There was a *tap-tap-tapping*, like mice in the roof.

'Aren't you gonna let me in?' wheedled someone on the outside.

You looked down into the palm of your other hand, lying on your knee. You were white-pale, trembling. You shifted your hips against the couch, willing the room to swallow you.

I was on my knees and by your side in a second, whispering 'Who is it?'

You couldn't say. Your wise mouth wouldn't open. You couldn't meet my eye. I looked on your bent head—on the locks of hair falling over your face—and wondered what this could mean.

The tinny scratches turned suddenly violent. Thud thud thud went a fist on the thick wood.

'Let me in!' The voice was deep now, demanding.

'Who's at the door?'

You turned red despairing eyes on me. Your voice was hoarse. 'Don't let him in.'

'Okay.' I was calm. I was serene. I took your cheeks between my hands and brought my face right up to yours. I whispered fiercely three times, 'I love you. I love you. I love you'—making the words holy with my deliberateness. They were an invocation. They were a solemn promise.

Then I went to the door and opened it.

On the step, one fist upraised to knock again, stood a

middle-aged man whom I disliked on sight. His face was whisky-weak. His eyes criss-crossed with vodka lines. His jowls descended to his collar. He wore a St Vincent de Paul suit, threadbare, faded in patches. He was a mass of flab, standing to unnatural attention. He was like a slug that had been on a deportment course.

He looked me up and down before he spoke. 'Hello.' He sounded like the stranger offering lollies in the playground. *Hello, little girl.* 'Where is he?'

I was relieved to find myself unafraid. 'He doesn't want to see you,' I said, crossing my arms, leaning against the door-post, barring the way.

'But I want to see him.' He threw the words over my shoulder into the house, aiming them at your invisibility like spitballs.

'Go away.' I was as unflinching as a fishwife. I looked him in the eyes. He wasn't my problem. He wasn't *my* nemesis. He wasn't *my* childhood nightmare, come gloating from the past.

He pursed his lips at me, blowing wet carp-kisses towards my face. 'Don't be like that,' he wheedled. I smelled sourness, old clothes, old man, alcohol. 'I just want to *see* him. I just want to say *hello.*' There was a pouting petulance to his words. He reminded me of an ageing drag queen.

'Look,' I said, mustering all the obstinacy in my face, 'you can either fuck off now, on your own. Or you can wait until after I call the police, and leave with them.' Some clinging vestige of a long-forgotten television drama made me add, 'Got it?'

'Oooh-hoooo.' His face mocked my stance: *Think you're tough, little girl?* But his fat fingers crawled into fists and the fists crept into his pockets, where it was safe. He shuffled backwards. Again he aimed words past me. 'I was just paying a *social call*.'

I was a stone bureaucrat, reading him his rights. 'Right. That's it. I'm calling the cops.'

I'd never said 'cops' before in my life.

This time, he took two steps backwards, to the edge of the porch. 'Okay, *okay*.' A high nervous giggle snaked out from between his big lips. 'Just tell him I said *hello*. If it's not too much *trouble*.'

He turned then, and ambled down the path. His back was insolent, his plump rear waggling ostentatiously. *Fine then, I'll go.* His steps, however, were hurried. His footsteps stuttered. One of his shoelaces trailed stupidly behind one of his shoes, like a string of tin cans rattling behind a hearse.

I shut the door firmly, and snapped the deadlock on.

In silent triumph, I went back to you. All hail the conquering hero.

You hadn't moved.

Kneeling, I said levelly, 'Okay.' I was so close that I could feel the warmth of your body on my face. I didn't touch you. 'Do you want me to leave you on your own for a bit?'

Still staring at your open hand, you shook your head. Just barely.

'I'll tell you what I want to do,' I said, my voice still level and sensible. 'I want to take you to bed and hold you all night.'

You crumpled, my darling, bobbing your face forwards onto your knee. A sob like a hiccup twitched you.

I saw you reduced and humiliated. Unaccustomed infant's sobs breached all your manliness. You shuddered and wheezed with them.

I saw you reduced to nothing and I exploited it for all it was worth. God forgive me.

'Come on. Stand up.' I knew the steps of the dance now. I was leading.

You stood like a trained chimp, and took my hand.

In respectful silence, I led you up the stairs.

In the bedroom, I stood you before me like a toddler, systematically undressing you. Suit shirt underpants fell unregarded to the floor. Standing before you—you still looked at the ground—I removed my own clothes as clinically as before a medical examination.

Then flinging back the covers I climbed into the bed, manhandling you down with me, and lay on my back. Pulling and poking, I arranged you above me, your face on my breast, and cemented you in place with the blankets. Arms and legs around you I enveloped you. I pulled the blankets over our heads, locking us together into the smallest darkest space two bodies could occupy.

My voice in that tiny cathedral was hushed and reverent. 'Do you want to tell me?'

I felt nothing, angel. I had just pulled a holy ritual out of the air, and I felt nothing. I was officiating at a sacred ceremony, and I felt *nothing*.

You told me, of course, almost immediately.

His name was Clarry. He was a distant uncle who'd stayed with your family twice, once when you were seven and once when you were ten. He'd come creeping, in a haze of whisky, down the corridor to your room. He'd paused like a boogeyman over your bed. Pulling back the covers, he'd touched your trembling skinny body with his fat hands.

I felt a little bit silly for you, listening to those honest revelations. I smirked with my brain.

'My love,' I said, tightening my grip with every limb. You

shuddered against me, the ancient horror re-awoken.

'My love.' I said it convincingly.

I said it, conveying, *There is nothing more I can say, but my love, my love.*

Holding this new, childed man, my mind ticked over rapturously with the fresh possibilities before me. The whole of you encircled by the whole of me. My spirit sang with a powerful ecstasy as you wept.

'What did he do?' My voice dripped with honeyed concern. I had to know specifics.

These were the most difficult words you'd ever had to utter. 'He never actually ... y'know.'

I see. Penetration did not take place. 'Oh, darling,' I wailed under my breath.

I called you 'my darling' or 'my love' with difficulty, like an honest man obliged to lie. The sweet names tried to stick in my throat, because you spoke them with such sincerity. But I forced them out. I had to.

'He made me hold ... it.'

Hand jobs. That's it? 'Oh, my baby.' My hands tightened on your sides, squeezing reassurance and support.

You choked it out. 'He said I had to ... in my mouth.'

Oh, darling, you were incoherent. Your tears soaked my shoulder. I was delirious. I was enchanted.

'My love,' I said. It was a litany, a mantra of false succour. 'My love. My love. My love.'

With racking sobs and fists contracting violently, like heartbeats, against my shoulders, you gave your pain to me. It trickled down over my skin. It came in wheezing at my ears. It fluttered desperately through my pupils. I took it and I shaped it to my pleasure.

I'm damned for that. My love.

We both fell asleep.

I shouldn't have had the duvet pulled up over myself. I always have weird dreams when I'm too hot.

It wasn't really a dream. More of an idea with a soundtrack.

The thumping on the door went through my head, the thud thud thud of a deliberate fist on hardwood. Inside this dream, this sweaty sleeping idea, a long thin line of panic spouted between my stomach and my head. I knew I was in trouble.

Thud thud thud, and it's me he's after.

Thud thud thud, and there's nowhere to hide.

And the idea that floated like a cloud of steam into my mind was this: it's *my* uncle out there, banging on the door. It's *my* uncle, gone to seed and smashing bottles. It's *my* uncle, come to claim me back for childhood and powerlessness.

Thud thud thud, on the wooden door.

It took me ages to wake up, even after I realised I was asleep and dreaming. I had to try and shake dead limbs, open sleeping eyes, think with a numb mind. I slipped in and out of the idea, trying to shrug it off. It lay all along me, pinning me to the bed so I couldn't move.

Finally some twitch of mine flicked the duvet off my upper body, and I woke up to a rush of cold air and silence.

You were sound asleep.

I sat up and put the bedlamp on. All my skin was pink and flushed and traced with creases to show how I'd lain. My hair stuck to the side of my face.

I sat very still and waited for the idea to dissipate completely.

I hardly ever thought about my uncle these days. As far as

I knew, he'd never made an effort to contact me. I was glad about that. I couldn't think of anything worse than having to speak to him, trying to address my convoluted self to that unasailable simplicity and worthiness. Trying to answer his elementary question: why?

I thought of him, crumpled at the kitchen table where I saw him last.

I don't doubt I've left some shadow on him: a bad taste in his mouth, a nervous twitch. I imagine he thinks of me when he reads the awful newspaper in the evening, and knows the world to be spinning too fast, skew-whiff.

You were edgy when you woke. At dinner, you talked and laughed with a slight manic intensity, eating barely a morsel.

You got up three times in the night after we went back to bed, pacing the house on mysterious errands. You sat up next to me, bedlamp blazing, reading instead of sleeping.

At midnight, I woke. Your eyes bored into the paper with furious concentration.

I put my hand on your knee. I kissed your side, at the spot where the skin stretched taut over your hip bone, showing delicate latticeworked veins.

Snapping the book shut, you wanted to know, 'Am I keeping you awake? Do you want me to read downstairs?'

A periwinkle clinging to your side, I deepened my kiss, drawing my arm around your waist.

In the crook of my elbow I felt you stirring. Looking up, I saw your eyes were closed, your face haggard, hollow-eyed, grey with anxiety.

I hypnotised you with my eyes.

At that moment, in that place, all the world seemed like an extension of my logical, scheming mind. All events and people were like chess pieces I set down where I chose.

I wanted you as you had been that afternoon—craven, reduced, abased. And with a tear and a swish of limbs through bedlinen, you were.

We reassumed our position of the afternoon. I took you into me. As you took up that familiar attitude, I asked in your ear, 'Is that better?'

Melodramatically husky, you confided, 'I feel very safe, here.'

I liked being your refuge, the only port in the storm. I put my hands on your slim flanks and told you, 'I feel safe, too.'

Uncle Clarry never turned up again.

I was disappointed. Protected by my knowledge of what he was, I could have fought him off endlessly. I daydreamed, for a little while, about coming home and finding him in the house, bailing you up against the wall. I'd force him off, trip him up, kick his fat face.

Then I'd gather you to me. I'd swallow you whole. I'd absorb you into my bloodstream, and you'd circle around inside me, endlessly.

Ruthlessly, I invented confidences of my own. I rejoiced at the strange blindness that let you take them in exchange for yours, like Monopoly money for real gold.

I lay in the submissive emotional position, curled against your chest with your reassuring arm around my waist, your hand on my head.

'I have dreams sometimes,' I said.

'You can tell me.'

'They're horrible.'

'It's all right.' Your big eyes promised to stand between me and any great horror.

'I dream ... that there's a *thing* in bed with me.' A pause, so you could wonder: What thing? I made my breath come heavily, squinting my eyes with the effort of speech.

'It's all burned,' I explained, squeezing your hand convulsively. 'All blackened.'

Another pause. You were intent, silent, your lips parted in concentration. You were willing me to be healed from this awful psychic scar. I was delighted.

I went on. 'I notice—just gradually—that this *thing* ... it's like, a big lump of melted plastic. All dripping. Shrivelled. It's awful. It's my *mother*.' I turned my face into your chest. I was crying real tears. I didn't feel anything. I don't know how I did that. Sometimes I surprise myself.

'Oh, darling,' you said, your hand on my head. You were quivering with the force of what I'd told you. 'Oh, my darling!'

You were enthralled. You were mine.

I pushed my advantage. 'And I wonder ... like, I wish I knew ... I can't remember the ... *crash* ...' I sniffed away the tears briskly, like someone well used to facing ingrained grief with stoicism. I was rewarded with that melting look, that flowing compassion of yours. 'But I wish I knew what was going through her mind as it happened.'

You spoke gently, the way that parents do when coating some truth in illusion to make it palatable to young children. 'She must have worried about you. She must have thought that she loved you very much and that she hoped someone would look after you.'

I found this thought distasteful. I hate feeling pity for people's vulnerability, their patheticness. It's too much of a liability. There are so many pathetic people.

I suppose she wasn't to know what I would be like. All babies are the same. But something in me thought irritably, More fool her.

'Oh, that's beautiful!' I exclaimed with sincerity. I angled my head upwards and kissed your thumb, smiling up at you from between your fingers. 'And now I've got you.'

I used to watch you sleep, every night.

I've always slept lightly. I always wake up at least two or three times in a night. Much more of late. I'm nearly completely insomniac.

But I loved waking up in the night when it meant I could watch you when you were alseep.

When you were awake you often moved jerkily. It could be quite frustrating. I'd have you in my sights, in some perfect pose, at an ideal viewing distance, with the light just right and your expression just exactly what I needed. And then you'd suddenly shift, shrug, scratch, sneeze; and the image would dissipate jaggedly away.

But asleep, you were much better. I could stare unreservedly, because you couldn't see me.

I savoured your face the most, the thing I could least afford to stare at too hard when you were awake. The curve of your nose, the hollows of your eyes, the tiny holes your beard squeezed itself out of. And the expressions! Naked, open, unguarded. Delicious. You'd dream anxiety and your face would pinch and crumple like a toddler's. You'd dream something funny and smile beamishly at the air. And your movements became slow and irregular with the heaviness of sleep. Your whole body was diffuse in the lamplight, like some Impressionist character all made of splodges.

I miss you terribly.

I lounge about in your dressing-gown, sometimes. It's too long for me. It trails on the floor behind me, and I have to gather the hems in my hands as I go down the stairs. I sit on the couch, drinking red wine from one of your long-stemmed glasses. I don't know if they're officially the correct glasses for wine, but they suit my purposes. I remind myself of an ancient, forgotten diva, who, denied the stage and love affairs with foreign royalty, employs her thwarted theatrical tendencies in kicking the cat and bullying the servants.

What do I miss? I miss losing myself in you. I was like the diva in her prime then, performing her most celebrated role, so passionately involved in her part that she lost herself entirely; or afterwards, whisked between lovers, received princes in boudoirs hung with red exotic drapery and studded with silver candlesticks.

I miss the blueness of the night-time bedroom and the bigness of the curtainless window and the silvered incandescence of your skin and mine. I miss the animal warmth of your body beside mine.

I remember (this breaks my heart) one morning—or several, everything blurs—when I woke before you did. You snored gently, your hands curled under your head, your hair arrayed in dishevelled kiss-curls over your forehead.

I made a sudden movement. You woke abruptly. Your eyes opened, and you saw my face opposite yours. You mumbled something incoherent. Your voice still had sleep in it. Out your arms stretched, like a reflex. Insistently, inarguably, you encircled me, pulled me to you, like an enormous baby searching single-mindedly for milk.

You were swollen with the necessity of immediate love-making, irrational with it; still groggy. You cleared your throat. 'Oh...' you said, as if beginning to explain: *Oh, by the way.* 'Um...' Nodding downwards, you indicated your dilemma, turning towards me unfeignedly big, pleading, hungry eyes.

I took you into me without a word.

'Oh, you're a dream,' you said between your teeth, as the convulsions of orgasm shook you (carnal, uncontrollable convulsions, like vomiting or shivering). 'You're a dream. You're a dream.'

Y ou always rang from work as soon as I got home.

I knew to expect these calls. They unfailingly came ten or fifteen minutes after I walked in the door, suggesting that you watched the clock over your desk, waiting for me to finish school. That was a good sign. I approved of that.

I used the fact, once or twice, for emotional mileage.

We sat coiled on the couch, watching the evening news.

'You always call me when I come home,' I commented.

'I get worried.'

'I'm not gonna die.' I shifted position—oh, how subtle I was!—so that you were forced to re-locate your hand further down my leg.

'You didn't answer once,' you said.

'I was having coffee!'

I'd been invited along after school with some acquaintances. It was one of those awkward, 'everyone standing here is going so we can't not invite you' things. I sat and sipped politely in a cafe for an hour. I spent the whole time wondering what you'd think when I didn't pick up the phone.

You hand tightened on my ankle. You said, 'I thought, That's it. She's gone.'

I waited tensely for those calls. Often, I sat right next to the telephone, just watching it. I always let you ring half a dozen times before I picked up the receiver. Then I tried to sound busy with something else while I spoke to you.

Usually, of course, I *was* busy. After school was snooping time.

I was a careful, thorough sleuth. I knew the importance of small clues—what you were reading; little things you mentioned; tiny, unconscious gestures.

I scoured your possessions with a secret agent's calm meticulousness, every afternoon before you got home from work. Your clockwork, nine-to-six routine was very useful. It's good when your quarry has habits you can rely on.

I went through your filing cabinet gradually and systematically. Each day I read your letters, both private and official. I knew the dates and details of your divorce, as well as the anguish it had caused you.

The filing cabinet in the study was like an extension of your brain that I could open and rifle through at any time. You filed the acrid letters from your ex-wife under *Miscellaneous*.

There were only a limited number of letters, of course. But finding them was just the start. I read them over and over again. I touched them like talismans, for luck, whenever I was alone in the house. My eyes searched automatically through the columns of words, seeking anything useful, any new idea that they inspired.

I continued to read the occasional journal you kept in the

school exercise book that lay in the top drawer of your desk, beneath a pile of ancient accounts. I used it to invent myself in the image you had of me. If you wrote that I was charmingly impulsive, I exaggerated my impulsiveness threefold, waving my hands in the air and talking too fast, as I demanded presents and explained crazy new ideas. If you said you were worried that I barely ate, I was careful not to let you see me snacking.

It was like researching an enemy country so as to build the most effective weapon for the terrain.

It was this thoroughness that led me to look for clues everywhere. Even under the mattress.

I'd never thought of looking there before, but one afternoon after I'd checked all your drawers mechanically, already knowing what I'd find, I ran my hand swiftly along between the mattress and the bed. I don't know why.

And there they were, in a crumpled manila envelope.

The telephone by the bed made me jump when it rang. I froze, as though I'd been caught stealing. I counted to ten under my breath, then answered it with the envelope in hand.

'Hello?'

'Hey, darling.'

'Hello!' Expertly, I caught the receiver under my chin, leaving my hands free to probe the envelope.

'You got home all right, then?'

The word *cunt* caught my eye. I nearly fainted with surprise, but I kept my part up perfectly.

'No. I got chased up a lamp post by a pack of rabid giraffes. It was terrible.'

I come into the room and she's touching herself, lying

on the bed with her legs spread and one hand trailing down towards her cunt.

'Don't be silly.'

'Mmmm.' I was astounded at what I'd found. I whinged, 'When'll you be home? I'm hungry.'

You chuckled indulgently. 'Are you? There's biscuits in the cupboard.'

'I'm hungry for stir-fry.'

'I'll be there soon. About an hour. Go and watch "Heartbreak High".'

'Okay.'

'I love you,' you told me, and hung up.

I stared at the papers in my hand.

These were like gold. What a find!

I read them speedily, scientifically, but my fingers shook.

She fingers herself and says, 'I was just thinking about you.'

I've still got them. I read them, occasionally. They make me guilty, but at least they remind me of you.

They're pornography, really.

That didn't shock me.

I'd read pornography—real, official pornography—before. It seemed stupid.

It was in a magazine that you had below your socks in a drawer. An ancient *Hustler*. You must have jerked off to it before you met me. I found it when we were still living in your old house. (Yes, darling, I was snooping even then.)

My first instinct had been to take offence, next time an

opportunity presented itself. An unworldly girl could easily get away with being disgusted at what I'd found. It was ideal guilt-inducing material.

In an instant, I had formulated a plan: I would become silent and withdrawn. I'd fiddle with things, abstracted, anxious. You'd worry:

'Baby? Baby?'

'Hmmmm? Sorry—I ...' A shake of the head.

Then, when you, in desperation, sought for the problem, I would snivel a little, I thought, and confess what I'd found, turning big troubled eyes on you, inviting reassurance. That should be good for nights of anxious, careful lovemaking on your part.

But after a moment or two of flicking through this magazine, I abandoned this idea. I thought instead how sad it was that a man of such intense, desperate passions should find himself masturbating in front of cheap glossy paper. I experienced a surge of sympathy for you, darling, for the ordinariness of those old arousals, the loneliness of them.

This fallibility, this little patheticness, I surmounted in an instant. If you were a slightly different shape to the one I'd been led to expect, that was okay. I'd just tailor myself around you.

It was two years out of date when I found it. I suppose this only demonstrates the sameness of those magazines.

The stories were all simple; too simple. There are only six or seven adjectives you can use when writing smutty porn. The same words crop up again and again: *hot, wet, thrust.* The women all seemed to have silly, dated sex-kitten names like Kimberly and Taylor.

They were powerful images, of course. Especially for one with my past.

I'll admit that my heart beat a little faster and my hands shook imperceptibly when I saw the pictures. But it was more the *idea* that such pictures existed, than the images themselves. All those splayed airbrushed thighs, those pink plastic fingernails, those shameless *cunts* shaved in funny bikini patterns, grated on me. I soon grew bored. Besides, the models seemed to have such terrible taste in shoes. It was all gold sandals, pink slippers, thigh-high leather fuck-me boots. How can you have elaborate, operatic fantasies about a woman wearing gold sandals? I wondered.

There were a few erect penises, but again, the men to whom they were attached left me cold.

I had hoped vaguely, after the initial shock passed, that the magazine would give me some ideas. Clues. I turned the pages with my usual professional detachment.

But I soon realised that these trite fantasies wouldn't do at all. They were nothing like as vivid, as charged, as the scenarios I created every moment and lived out with you.

I smoothed it shut, and tucked it back underneath the socks, where it belonged.

But your own writings were different. They were personal. They were like private poetry; too exquisitely ridiculous to be read aloud.

I perused my treasure silently, speedily, braiding it in with my picture of you as I went.

You had never used words like *cunt* and *cock* and *cum* to my face. Whenever I swore—'Fuck!'—you shook your head, more lover-injured than parent-angry. And yet here those harsh guttural words jumped out like splashes of red across the white page, impossible to ignore or excuse.

They aren't calm and sensible and well ordered like all your other correspondence. The writing is messier, too. They're fragmented—a paragraph on a scrap of tracing paper, a page torn from a notebook covered front and back—all savagely wrinkled with the force of your furtiveness as you shoved them into the envelope.

They're like a kind of shorthand. They're something you knew already, but took a deep pleasure in articulating.

I tell her to do it harder. She obeys.

The scenarios were already there in your mind, before you ever took up a pen. They've burned holes, they've been sitting there for so long.

I stand at the foot of the bed and just watch.

They're like my pictures.

You were never as thoroughly bad as me, of course. Your fantasies, compared to my discarded ones, were almost tame. They bordered on the normal, though they had more bite than the everyday, the long-married. I couldn't imagine my uncle whispering such things—

I tell her that I'm going to fuck her harder than I ever have before. She's scared and I have to hold her legs apart.

—to my fat indifferent aunt.

Seeing these deeper desires—scrawled as intensely as I had

once scribbled the outlines of my victims on expensive sketch paper—parading across the pages, made my mouth dry with a powerful, psychological lust.

I wanted to hear you confess your desires. I wanted to see you shiver and almost break before the weight of acknowledgement.

It wasn't your fault, what happened.

I provoked you, knowing what provocation would reveal. You were a scorpion I poked and prodded into stinging me.

It's funny how lusts don't seem to exist for you in your other secret world, in your journal. Nothing else is taboo in there. You confess to worrying you'll go bald; to fearing impotence; to hating yourself; but *never* to these desires. They're segregated from the rest of your secrets, in their manila envelope. They're like a limb you've tried to amputate.

And that's so terribly good of you that it brings tears to my eyes.

You were prepared to be a gentle man. Civilised, you had succeeded in subordinating your sadistic desires. They didn't fit in with your picture of humanity, and so you fought them down, lulled them into an uneasy slumber at the bottom of your consciousness.

I woke them. I did it deliberately.

Once, I read a magazine article about sadomasochism.

You can't guess, it said, under which neat lawn in this city lies the dungeon.

And I wondered about the anonymous man they'd interviewed, living above the dungeon. Were there times when, changing his socks or buttering toast, he forgot about the chamber under his feet and the racks and the whips and the manacles and the Internet site and the coded advertisements in obscure magazines? Or were his very footsteps charged with sexual significance, as he strolled about over the realisation of a fantasy?

Did he ever long to move house, to go somewhere innocuous, some house where there were no concrete neuroses buried beneath the kitchen tiles?

I did more than build a simple house around my fantasies. I built a whole artificial self.

I've realised now, too late, that sexual fantasies are fictions. Trying to make them real is like trying to converse according to an opera score.

I can't stand violence.

I close my eyes in graphic movie scenes.

I can't bear to see sadism made flesh. I hate booted feet belting into stomachs, blood dripping down foreheads, gunshots, stabbings, punches, slaps.

It's the *risk* that bothers me, I think. The risk of pain, to the hitter, the kicker, the shooter of guns. I can't bear the thought of risking myself, of leaving myself open to reciprocal attacks. I hate the way victims can so easily get up and retaliate, in the movies. So, for some funny twisted reason, my sympathy latches irrevocably onto anyone who's being hurt. I feel every blow. I wince and wince. My friends used to piss themselves laughing at the way I closed my eyes in horror movies, protecting my neck from the vampire with one hand.

In all my imagined violences, I existed only as a thin thread of control. I was all mind, in those fantasies, barely present save to shape and direct the responses of my victims.

I'm starting to do weird things, here on my own.

I've heard that if you deny yourself all stimuli—block your ears, cover your eyes—you can excite your mind to hallucinations. Visions.

I bought ear-plugs from the chemist's.

I no longer give a damn how I appeared to any other living being. The chemist's assistant might have glanced at me with hostile curiosity as she handed me the change. She might have raised her eyebrows, affronted, at my arsenic-white face, and my red, sunken eyes. I wasn't even looking.

Back in this room, I made myself blind with an ancient airline eyemask. I bottled the sound of my rushing blood, stoppered my ears with twists of wax.

In the void, I waited.

I expected avenging angels, terrible seraphs pointing accusatory swords, the pure light of vengeance in their eyes. I expected monsters: the demons swimming at the bottom of my subconscious, come up at last for air.

I expected to be judged.

Nothing happened. Thin tears oozed at the corners of my eyes. I resisted the urge to squash them away with one finger.

I fell into an uneasy sleep.

I hate being here without you.

I spent an unspecifiable age, last night, staring at the air in front of the white wall of our bedroom.

My eyes hovered in some focusless hinterland and I saw coloured shadows, dancing. Once or twice a cloud of yellow and some spots of reddish-black coalesced. They seemed to become a hand, sitting in repose as if in a lap; or an eye, blinking and looking to one side, avoiding my gaze.

I could not make you real. I didn't learn you as you learnt me, with the meticulousness of passion. Of love.

You said you could make me again, out of the air.

I know what you meant now, when in the shower you put your hands on my shoulders and turned me full circle.

Blinking through the steam, your thumbs on my collarbones, you confided, 'I know *every inch* of this.'

The hot water brought your blood to the surface in blotches. Rivulets ran down your red face. As if to demonstrate the truth of your words, you skimmed your hands over my shoulders, my neck, my cheeks, my arms, hands, waist.

You said, 'If you disappeared, I could make you again, out of the air.'

Fishing in my false heart, I hooked false comforts and offered them to you, earnestly. 'I won't *disappear*! I'm not *going* anywhere!'

And you, misguided visionary, looked into my treacherous eyes, and saw nothing amiss.

'You're beautiful,' you told me. The words broke, passing the lump in your throat.

I didn't seek those pages out again for days. I buzzed with the secret knowledge of what I'd read. I kissed you, talked with you, squeezed your hand in the street, thrilling every moment with a strange expectant nervousness.

Carefully, carefully, I prepared myself for the final assault.

I sugared my lips with cherry-flavoured lip balm. I washed my hair in coconut shampoo. I smothered myself in cheap teenage scent, till I reeked of strawberries.

'You always smell the same underneath,' you told me.

I laughed. 'What're you trying to tell me? I should shower more often?'

'No, it's that childish smell.' I felt your nostrils flare on my shoulders as you inhaled. 'Babies. Milk.'

After that, I was careful to have milk more often. I left on my face the traces of it that clung round my lips after drinking. I rubbed it into my skin like perfume.

I made my first move at one of our picnics.

It was your idea entirely. It was you who loved picnicking under the huge spreading tree in our backyard. It was you who made the sandwiches and folded the tartan blanket for me to sit on.

I've never really liked *weather*. Being outside could be good, if it meant solitude. If it left me alone with my dark thoughts. If it freed me from the pin-pricks of guilt that human contact engendered.

I used to hate it, for example, if my aunt came up and offered to make me a sandwich when I sat at the kitchen table, daydreaming. I'd always shake my head and disappear out the back door, to be alone. I hated to have human decency and my mind in the same room at the same time.

But rain, wind, sun ... they smacked too much of cleansing, sandpapering forces, abrasive against my secret thoughts.

Outside's too *big*, as well. I preferred the safe spaces of the little burrows you and I made beneath blankets. Even with the curtains drawn, there was always enough light to see your face.

So all that time, as I giggled and threaded daisy chains (how charming, how adorable!) I was slightly uncomfortable. But like a true opportunist, I was able to work under any circumstances.

I wore jeans, rolled up at the ankles; and one of your white work shirts, far too big. Through the thin cotton, the black shadow of my bra was obvious. My feet were bare, so that you could tickle the instep.

We sat on the cool grass in the deep shade of the biggest tree. When we'd finished with the food, we pushed the bones of sandwiches and the dead husks of salads to one side.

I yawned expansively. 'Can I lie on you?'

That wry, through-the-nose laugh, as though I kept asking, in my naiveté, *Can I give you a million dollars?*

'Of course.'

I settled my head on your outstretched legs, near the top of them. I looked up at the leaves. I felt a creature come crawling over my ankle. 'Ugh!' I squealed. 'There's something on my leg!'

Indulgently, you reached out. 'Where is it?' You searched with your hands over my two calves, flicking the unseen little legs away. 'There. It's gone.' You didn't move your hand, however, but left it motionless, a big solid warmth on my skin.

'No,' I said, wriggling. 'There's still something there.'

'Oh, there is *too*!' Your fingers drummed on my ankle. 'It's a huge big *spider*!'

'Yuck! Get it off!'

You walked the spider over my jeans, over my belly, until you held me awkwardly round the waist.

'What *is* this? Spiders don't do this.'

'This one does.'

'Oh!' I was tired of boring euphemisms, silly games. I wanted to hear you declare yourself again. 'What do you want to do, spider?'

Your lips against my ear blew hot breath as you whispered, 'I want to run my hands all over you. I want to feel your skin under my fingers.'

I made you go further. 'What else?'

'Pinch your nipples.' Your eyes were closed. You swallowed.

This was getting close. I watched you keenly, through narrowed eyes. 'What else?'

'Unzip your jeans and put my hand down them and—' You gave a short embarrassed laugh. 'I'm not getting carried away …? You're not offended?'

'What else?' I pulled your hand up under my shirt. Your hand splayed, inoffensive, on my belly. You laughed nervously, not meeting my eyes.

I pulled my shirt off.

'Hey!' You glanced around, as though expecting to see hordes of respectable citizens come charging over the walls armed with pitchforks.

'No-one can see us.'

You snorted through your nose, shaking your head. 'Crazy girl!'

I pulled your head down until your face hovered over my breasts. 'Is that what you want?' I asked, sweetly.

And you made no reply, but only stared, overwhelmed.

*

I have a recurring dream.

I'm lying in a hospital bed. At the same time, I'm watching the action as though it were a film: I'm an invisible presence. My uncle and aunt are there, and a well-meaning delegation of girls from St Mary's. They're all standing around awkwardly, trying to make conversation, feeling terribly sorry for me.

There's been a shocking accident. I'm terribly afflicted. I've gone blind, or lost my legs, or had my face all scalded away. These injuries are always very graphic. I see the bleeding stumps of my legs, the scarred hollows where my eyes were, the red monstrosity my face has become.

Eventually one of my visitors breaks down, and blurts out, 'Oh, it's terrible! What a dreadful thing to happen!'

And the me-in-the-bed thinks about this, and I say, 'Oh, it's no more than I deserve.' There is a feeling of calmness, of things having come to a conclusion, like the end of a film. The statement seems a fair summing-up. *Oh, it's no more than I deserve.*

It occurs to the me-that-floats-unseen, the disembodied observer, that this statement is more dreadful than the accident which has befallen me. There is a sense of tragedy, and I feel like weeping.

We ended up inside, as I'd hoped. You carried me there, cupping my neck and knees over your forearms. There was a strange, magnetised distance in your eyes, and your footfalls were slow and deliberate as you climbed the stairs. I could feel your arms through your shirt. They were scorching hot, as though the skin was sunburnt, as though your shirt would ignite.

You laid me like a doll on the bed, kissing me fiercely on the forehead.

Removing my clothes, you were as careful as usual, but somehow less tender. Kneeling between my legs, removing my jeans, you met my gaze. Your eyes were burning. You looked over me, at every inch, holding my knees. You were biting your lip and your hands trembled. You seemed to have to concentrate very hard on every breath you took.

I smiled serenely, like the Madonna. I had read in a journal of psychology that an important part of the Lolita Complex was the need to violate innocence.

'Come on,' I said, quietly.

And then you were above me.

With a terrible thrill, I realised what I'd so easily wrought. There was such a suppression of violence in your touch that I nearly flinched, I nearly fainted. Your fingers were light against my skin, but you were being consumed with desperation.

You bit at my neck, with the sharp points of your teeth. Those pin-pricks were the beginning of all this, weren't they?

You felt your way down my neck with lips clamped tight over teeth, leaving a snail-trail of spittle which flared coldly on my skin.

Your sharp teeth clamped sharper than usual into the soft skin around my nipple. Taken genuinely by surprise, I gasped in pain.

'Oh! I'm sorry, baby!'

The skin on my breast throbbed sharply with the pain. 'It's okay.' It always hurt, when you did that.

'I never know when to *do* that!' You sounded miserable. 'Sometimes you seem to like it. But sometimes I get it wrong.'

I made a mental note to be more consistent with my reactions.

Then, judging my moment perfectly, willing you full of that need, I moved as though to roll away from underneath you.

I saw you struggle with yourself and start to lose.

'No,' you said, or made a noise that meant no. And you held my wrists together, with one hand.

With your feet, you hooked my legs apart.

Your face shone with sweat. Your eyes, sheathed over with an animal intensity of purpose, were on my face. You bit your lip, concentrating, as your body arced and dipped above me.

I lay supine, my thin wrists tacked to the bed under the iron span of your right hand. I knew a moment of the most intense, stifling, true panic when I realised that *I couldn't move.* I couldn't make you stop without crying out. A shout or a whimper at that moment would, I knew, have shattered the careful connection I'd wrought between us.

I couldn't close my eyes, chew my lip, give any sign that I was taking a punishment. Your bulging eyes were inches from my face. Any indication of dismay would break the spell, leave you scrambling off me, apologising, reduced, afraid to come near me. Perhaps you would even be revolted by the urges my flimsy body had awakened in you.

You lowered your hips. I could feel rough hair on my thighs. You used your left hand to find my entrance. I felt your knuckles on my belly and your knees between my calves. It seemed as though a grim doom were upon me.

Pictures came to me in vivid flashes, as bright against my confusion as fireworks against a cloudy sky. I saw my hideous gallery, my debauched harem. They came parading before me, mocking, scornful. My mind shrieked against the possibility that I, the controller, the cracker of whips, the giver of orders, should find myself here, open, without hope. I braced myself against discomfort and humiliation.

And then, as you entered, I saw as though in a vision all those thousands of black-and-white, faceless women: legs spread, entered, debased, attacked. Every single one of them raised her face to me, and on her face was a smile. And I saw in a second the features of those faces, which I had thought were so carefully copied from life. I saw how exactly they resembled my own face, cut up and scattered among them all, so that one had my nostrils and another the corners of my eyes. *We're your creatures*, they seemed to say. *You live through us. You are one of us.*

And you plunged into me, and I felt a desperate contracting deep inside, an urgent, shivery palpitation. I gasped for air. I was stifled, but drawn hopelessly on. It was like drowning in a river full of rapids. It was like suffocating in a black hole.

I lost the ceiling above to a sudden spattered sand-blindness, as though my eyes had fainted. I lost myself to a formless humming in my ears, a dizzying inchoate rushing.

It was the most profoundly satisfying thing that I had ever experienced.

'Phew!'

'Hmmm.' I kissed your head, a reflex motion. My lips met hair and I thought how like kissing an animal it was.

'Well, that's a new one!' You were human again, good-humoured.

'Yep.'

'Did you like that?' There was a faint note of disbelief in your voice. It was overlaid with more obvious concern, as well as the post-coital chattiness with which lovers attempt to re-establish everyday, verbal contact.

'Yes,' I said. I was tingling all over, exhausted and invigo-rated.

Rolling over, propping your head on one hand, you asked, 'You weren't ... put off, or anything?'

'No.' I smiled lovingly. 'Let's do it again.'

It took an hour, I knew, between one time and the next.

I covered your hips with the sheet. I didn't like to see that flaccid thing lounging shrunkenly between your legs. It made you seem too much a creature made of the same stuff as me.

A sudden high-pitched concern flooded your voice. 'What've I done?' You stroked my breast gently, your eyebrows twisted with worry.

'It's all right.' Magnanimously, I forgave you the smarting, the sharpness.

'Oh, baby!' You measured the extent of the damage between your thumb and forefinger. 'I'm so sorry.'

Afterwards, a deeper, duller pain replaced the initial sting. Looking into the mirror, I saw a dark spreading bruise. Against the carefully guarded whiteness of my skin, it came as a shock. Then I realised that it was your mark, a tangible record of your passion.

When you saw it again, you clicked your tongue in disap-proval.

I wore it with pride, observing it carefully each night until it faded away.

It was a kind of game; but you wouldn't speak of it, outside the ring.

I experimented with disconcerting bluntness.

'Wow!' I said, after another of the slightly dangerous sexual encounters had left me breathless and bruised. 'I'd never imagined it could be so *good*!'

But you did not reply. Chewing your lip savagely, you lowered the lids of your eyes halfway, irritated.

So I had to encourage you in silence, with signs and signals.

It became my delicate business to seem modest, good and vulnerable, while doing my best to encourage your basest instincts. So I'd get changed with my back to the open door, pretending I had no idea that you were standing in the doorway. Absorbed in my homework, sprawled out on the lounge room floor, I'd absently scratch my stomach, lifting my shirt higher than was necessary; then laugh a little, blushing, as though I'd just realised that you were watching.

In bed, I read. You lay on your back beside me, your hands behind your head, thinking. It was a very hot night. We had the window open, but no air moved through it.

'I wish there'd be a storm,' I told you suddenly, tossing my book shut onto the bedside table.

'Mmmm.'

'I'm hot!' I threw the sheet back off my body, pointing my toes towards the ceiling.

'Me too.'

I blew on your face, and you smiled, abstractedly. I liked that abstracted smile of yours, when you thought you were worrying about something too important for me to understand and I did something cute and naive.

'God, it's boiling!' I sat up, cross-legged. 'Excuse me,' I

said, taking off the sleeveless shirt I used as an improvised pyjama-top.

'Hey!'

'It's okay,' I placated you. 'I'm decent.'

'No you're not!' You looked irritated and tired. '*I* wear pyjamas.'

'So do I!' I held out the waistline of my boxer shorts to demonstrate. It was my unashamed-primeval-nakedness persona. '*You* sleep topless! So now we're the same.' I yawned expansively, as though yawning took up all my attention and I had forgotten all about my body. 'I just want to be like you.'

I quite like this irritable prudishness in you. It meant that I was having an effect. Driving *you* to hypocrisy was quite an achievement.

I leant over to kiss your forehead and smooth your hair with my hand, pretending that the proximity of my breasts to your eyes was the last thing on my mind.

There was the faintest tightening of the muscles in your face, a creasing around your eyes and a tension in your jaw, that showed me what I was doing was working.

You took a shallow apprehensive breath, trying to ignore your arousal. But on your face there were these little downwards flicks of your pupils, that betrayed the little worried calculations taking place behind them. I could see you wondering whether it would be plausible to pull the sheet over yourself. It was unbearably erotic.

I pulled the sleepy-little-girl act, snuggling up to your side and burying my face in your neck. I willed my cheeks to expand and soften, my lips to become big and unconsciously red, like the lips of a child startled from sleep.

You smiled a little in acknowledgement of my gesture. I

saw through one of my falsely heavy eyelashes that you were reluctant to move.

'Gimme a cuddle,' I demanded sleepily, with just a touch of sulkiness.

Then you were obliged to turn your body towards mine, weren't you? and when you held me stiffly, holding yourself away from me so that there was a centimetre's open air between us, I wriggled forwards, closing the gap. I seemed already half-asleep; it seemed a somnambulist's movement. There was nothing you could do.

Long seconds later, I felt your fingers along my cheek and your sibilant whisper: 'Are you asleep?'

In answer, I kissed you, still feigning half-sleep. I yawned into your mouth.

You moved downwards, kissing the tops of my breasts, regarding my face cautiously every moment. I cast narrow sleepy eyes at you, moving my back against the sheet as though settling into a more comfortable position for sleep. You kissed my belly hard, your chin scraping my navel.

And now I seemed to wake with a certain surprise. I breathed in sharply and raised my arms above my head, stretching, guiding you further down my trunk than I think you had intended to go.

Before you quite knew what was happening, I had, through a series of opportunistic wriggles, manoeuvred you off the bed entirely, so that you stood, all dazed and burning, on the floor. I guided your hands to the hems of my shorts, and smiled as though at a bright dawn when you tugged them down over my feet and off.

My lower half dangled off the bed. My legs cast about in the air like tentacles. Like tentacles, I wound my arms up and around your neck. A sea anemone closing around my prey, I manoeuvred you inside me.

You thrust a few times, unobtrusively, your mouth open against my shoulder in a toothless, impotent bite.

I didn't want things getting routine. You weren't allowed to just *have* me, just like that. Without displays, oaths, tears, turmoil.

I turned my mouth to your ear. I asked you, very quietly, 'You gonna fuck me, darling?'

It was a challenge. Go on. Prove yourself.

'Mmmm,' you said, quickening your pace a little, digging your toes into the carpet.

It wasn't enough.

'Do it harder.'

I must make it clear—I didn't want you to do it harder for any *sexual* reason, not today. I just knew by instinct that to seem aroused by dominance and aggression would serve to disconcert you. And a disconcerted man was easier to control.

'Do it harder.' To emphasise my point, I opened my legs wider. Come on. Be a man.

I felt you tense. Okay then. You straightened up, with me still wrapped around you like a monkey. I felt you scrabbling at my clasped hands, undoing them. You laid me down flat on the bed. I sat half up, resting on my elbows.

You twisted your fingers into my hair. It didn't hurt. It was satisfying, like scratching an itch. Your face was scarlet. Your breath came in convulsions. Your cheeks were taut red spheres. The light of battle was in your eyes.

Bending your wrist, you made me look down, between our bellies. You rested your sweat-slicked forehead on mine, looking down also. We watched my triangle of duck's down.

We regarded my open legs.

'*See that?*' you hissed, desperately. 'You *see that?*' I saw you enter me, again and again.

'Mmm,' I said shortly under my breath: a timid assent.

In my heart, I crowed with triumph.

How is it that, beneath you, under you, ruled by you, penetrated by you, I revelled in my victory?

By arousing a passion that you were a slave to, I had won an easy mastery. I had demanded an offensive, and made myself the commander. Your manhood—this grunting, sweating masculinity—was a gift that only I could bestow.

You tensed, you went rigid, you bit your lip.

'I'm gonna *come*. I'm gonna come in *you*.' The words were so laboured as to be hardly comprehensible. And I lay there and looked as your eyes scrunched up and your mouth opened like a fish's and you whimpered and you ejaculated.

You were all, all mine.

You hated being tickled, though you tickled me all the time.

I'm not especially ticklish, though I still don't really like being tickled.

I used to tickle you to make you tickle me. It was a game with a slight power-edge to it, because you really were bigger and stronger than me.

I remember once I made you pin me to the ground, just by tickling you relentlessly as we watched the news together.

'Don't!' you admonished, slapping my hand away again and again.

I kept on trying, until finally you stood up and crossed the room.

'What?' I was in my naughty toddler mood, standing behind you in an instant, reaching under your arm, blatantly tickling as you tried to shrug my hand away.

Stooping over, you shoved your hands into your armpits, crossing your arms over your stomach. 'No, really,' you appealed to me sadly from beneath your hunch. 'I really don't like that.'

'I'm not,' I said, tickling you again.

'Don't!' You wriggled absurdly, trying to escape me. I stroked my fingers, feather-light, down over your stomach.

And then you stretched your arms out and before I knew it you had both my forearms in your grasp. You felled me easily. I lay with my back against the rug.

'Haha! Pinned!' you crowed. I jerked under your weight, lips pursed in an appearance of determination. You grinned down at me. 'Pinned and not liking it!'

My wrists tingled. Your fingers were tight bracelets. I lay as if exhausted, as if gathering my strength for another struggle. I wasn't tired at all.

I must have looked pretty piteous.

'Oh!' You were gently anguished. 'I *want* to let you up.' You laid your head on my stomach, holding your spine stiffly so that you didn't rest all your weight on my midriff. I arched my back, squishing my belly into your cheek. You explained: 'I just don't want you to tickle me.'

I said nothing, jutting my chin resolutely. I rejoiced in the strength of your grip, in my genuine inability to move. The rest of the world was blissfully removed as an option. I had nowhere to go but deeper into you.

*

Sometimes you surprised me.

I'd been used to waking to find you propped on one elbow, staring down at me, drinking my sleeping child's features greedily.

I used to glimpse you through narrowed eyes, while pretending to still be asleep. Then I could control my twitches and stretches and half-yawns. One arm flung above my head, I could ensure that my unconscious body showed itself to you, while my little heart seemed innocent of all manipulation. I could be certain that, at the end of the performance, you'd desire me.

That morning was different.

I was oblivious, then I seemed to dream you pressed hotly against me, clutching, desperate. I was nowhere, then I was under you, soaked in sweat, the sheet damply twined around my ankles. Your mouth was wide over mine. Patches of moisture gathered at the corners of my lips.

Each breath you took hurricaned hotly in my ear. Your arm around my neck haltered me as I tried to twist away from that uncomfortable, too-sudden assault. Your hand ran roughly along my leg, seeking to weasel between my knees.

I was taken aback. Being awake without my wits, my precious schemings, was like going out without clothes on.

You rolled onto me. I could hardly breathe under the weight of you. The heat in the air caught in my lungs like water vapour.

I didn't wriggle against you for long. I was awake, you were aroused, everything was as it should be. But I wasn't ready for you. All my gasps and sharp breaths were afterthoughts only. It hurt when you took me. I had your face to watch, and that was good, but it *hurt*.

And then came the day's best prize, which chased all

concern for pain far from my mind.

'Um—' you sobbed, sweating, gasping, driving—'sorry!'

I had thought there could be no pleasure more exquisite than that of seducing a shy man. But this debauching of a decent one was more compelling than anything I had ever experienced. The expressions I used to catch on your face! The naked desire was always chased quickly away by your luscious, sensuous shame. I grew taut with desire when I saw you close your eyes, trying to draw on some inner strength that wasn't there. I imagined what you'd be thinking: She's only a girl. Be careful. Be gentle. Restrain yourself. But of course, when I desired it desperately enough, I could always overcome that resolve. I delighted in the weakling that lust made of you.

I grew less and less interested in the world.

I couldn't do my schoolwork. I mean, I literally *could not do* maths or essays. I could hardly read. My mind kept wandering. I'd look at my homework, in the evenings, and then my attention would just slide off it. Sitting cross-legged on the floor at your feet, books open on my lap, I wormed with desire.

If I sat still for too long, alone in the room, I got dizzy. My ears were filled with a noise like static. If I closed my eyes, the static got louder. I felt sick. My stomach felt as though I were in an elevator, falling jerkily. I suppose it was because I didn't eat enough.

I couldn't eat much. My stomach wouldn't let me. It was like being nervous all the time. Eating seemed like inferior sensuality. Why should I put lukewarm noodles in my mouth when I could be kissing you?

Everything I touched felt clammy, except you. I didn't even like doing up my buttons or tying my shoelaces. There was a sheen on me like Vaseline. Everything felt coarse, sticky, except your skin. Maybe I was imagining it. But my hands sweated, even though they were cold. I sweated all over.

There was a kind of itch over all my skin. It could only be relieved by contact, by rubbing, by rhythmic touch. I think that's how cats' heads feel. It's why they move their necks the way they do, against your leg.

My breathing became shallow and incomplete. When I stood still, I swayed slightly. I sometimes thought I was hyper-ventilating.

I was sick. I was mad. I was like someone in love.

In Art, I was supposed to be working on my major painting. I couldn't concentrate. I stared into nothing, mentally creating situations for the two of us, instead. Absently, I painted my hands, just delicately dabbling the brush against my fingers. I traced broken bracelets on my wrists.

I forgot to wash it off.

At home, when you saw my hands, you said, 'We'd better get you cleaned up before dinner.' Taking me by the wrist, you led me into the bathroom.

Giving me baths had become a routine. You used to enjoy clucking at me when I splashed water out onto the tiles. You'd squat, fully dressed, by the side of the bath, pursing your lips with officious concentration as you soaped each limb in turn.

You turned the water on, and then went to check the pasta you were cooking.

I took off my clothes. I noticed splashes of paint on my knees. I made kissing faces at the mirror. I twisted seductively against the air.

I turned the cold tap off completely, and let the white tub fill with water that was far too hot. When the water was lapping halfway up the tub, I stepped inside.

My feet felt as if they were burning, at first. I stayed very still, as any movement of the water against my skin made it too hot to bear. Slowly, slowly I lowered myself down. I glowed pink. It hurt like sunburn. It made me urinate a tiny bit, involuntarily.

You bustled back in, wiping your hands briskly on your shirt, and reached for the floating sponge.

'Ow! That's too hot!' You sucked your fingers like a toddler.

'I like it,' I said, reclining like a mermaid, sinking my shoulders underneath. The sharp sting was sweet.

'You'll burn!'

I was feverish. Desire like maggots consumed me. The hot water made me shiver.

'It's fine.' I held one arm out imperiously, dangling my dirty hand. 'Come on.'

Shaking your head, you soaped me up, rubbing at the paint.

The heat made my nerves expand. Your touch felt fuzzier but more real. Through the steam, I watched you concentrating on your task. You bit your lip, like you did when you were driving in the rain.

I splashed at you, giggling. The water made big dark maps on your blue shirt. You recoiled. 'Shit!' The heat shocked you. 'It's all over the *floor*!' you cried.

'I'm sorry.' I was so drunk that it was hard to sound sincere. I giggled again.

You regarded the wet floor on either side with impotent dismay. 'You can be so *selfish*,' you muttered.

'I didn't mean to get the floor!' I cried in protest, before subsiding into giggles once more. 'I was trying to get *you*!'

Your pursed face collapsed, after that. You couldn't do anything but smile in reluctant indulgence, and kiss the crown of my head.

Languorously, I regarded my pink body. 'I'm hairy,' I said.

'You're perfect,' you replied, briskly rinsing my arm.

I fetched one of your disposable razors down off the sink. 'Give me the soap.'

I lathered my leg, pointing the toe. While you watched, I began to scrape away the hairs.

I didn't mean to cut myself. I was watching your trousers out of the corner of my eye.

'Shit!' you cried. It was as though I'd sliced *your* leg open under the knee. 'Be careful!'

It wasn't such a big cut. Maybe five centimetres across. But it was clean and crisp and blood welled up immediately.

'Are you all right? Should I get a band-aid?'

'Doesn't hurt,' I said. At first, it didn't.

I caught a look in your eyes, a surreptitiousness like guilt. Pink, bloody water flowed over my shin, into the tub. I lowered my leg until the cut was underwater. It hurt then, hotly, pulsingly. I drew my breath in between my teeth.

The water between my legs was murky. The colours of the paint and blood had all dissolved together, settling to the bottom. I eyed you from inside this greying, steamy bath. I was like a creature who belonged to another element. 'Kiss it better?' I asked, making the kissing face that I'd been practising in the mirror.

You obeyed. I was high on steam and on the curve of your

neck as you bent your head.

I think you sucked my blood. Your eyes were big and pup-pyish. Your fringe stuck to your face. You clamped your mouth across the cut as though you could bandage it with your lips.

'Come in,' I whined. You submitting, peeling your shirt and trousers off clumsily. Your lips were parted. You were so pow-erfully focussed that you forgot to bite your lip.

You planted your feet between my knees.

'Ssss!' you went, at the sudden heat.

The redness crept up your legs, between the hairs.

I pulled at your knees. 'Come down.'

You crouched. I closed my hot palm around your penis, pulling very gently.

Then I had you.

You had your eyes closed, and on your face there was this expression of tense concentration. I thought this must be what you'd look like masturbating. It was such a wonderful sight that I didn't want to blink. I held my eyes wide open until the tears came sliding out of them.

'I'm gunna!' you said. 'I'm gunna!' And then just as you came, I jerked you down and forward. You slipped and almost lost your balance. Flailing for the side of the bath, you immersed your balls in the hot water.

'*Jesus!*' The word was high and girlish. Your stomach twitched violently as you finished coming.

'Sorry,' I said, smiling with narrowed eyes.

'Oh, Jesus!' you said, your voice subsiding into a sigh.

I drank in the last precious moments of stillness, as you breathed deeply, head bowed, trying to retain your poise.

Then I pulled the plug out, sending blood and paint and sperm all spiralling away.

*

I made you conquer me, darling. I set bait you could not refuse.

'I need you so terribly,' I'd make you confess, night after intimate night. I cultivated in you an addiction for me, a physical dependency.

With the movements of my body, which you still assumed were spontaneous, uncontrived, I hypnotised you. I led you a slow, terrible dance. I became more dangerously passive, day by day. I retreated further and further, enticing you after me, into my personal inferno. And like the good, trusting man you are, you came always stumbling after.

Your guilt was still a powerful enemy. It was immensely strong in you. At times—like when I tried tickling your crotch as you read to me and you slapped my hand away—saying, 'Stop that!'—I feared I'd never be able to overcome it.

You tried to fight my onslaught in many ways. I could only conjure the demon in you every so often. I had to put up with hours of gentle, sincere lovemaking from you, in order that you wouldn't get suspicious. I lay there and let you tickle me with kisses.

Your overwhelming concern for my sexual pleasure began about this time. You were awkward about discussing it, at first. 'Do you ...' you said. 'Are you? I mean, is it ... okay? For you?'

'Of course!' I reassured you. I stayed very still, hoping that the top I'd just put on wouldn't rearrange itself as I moved around and ride upwards, covering the specifically calculated area of cleavage I had decided to display.

'I mean,' you went on wretchedly, 'you're very young. You know, sometimes couples have to *work* at. I mean. I mean. Is there anything you'd like to try?'

I demurred. I denied. I rejected the idea that I wasn't satis-fied. I scratched the top of my chest pointedly, to draw atten-tion to the visible tops of my breasts, and smiled a charming invitation.

Half an hour later, the cleavage had done its work. But you still insisted, rather awkwardly, on going down on me.

You'd done it before. I found it hard to contain my bore-dom. 'Mmmm,' I said. 'That's lovely.' And I stretched out my arms to you, beckoning you upwards, away.

'You're not getting bored, are you?' I inquired, trying not to sound too hopeful.

'I could do this all *day*,' you assured me.

I saw only your pixie's eyes between my knees, surrounded by the wrinkled skin that suggested you were grinning.

I smiled fondly down at you, to mask my own boredom.

In the end, however, I managed to harness your concern for my purposes.

It was just a matter of turning your generous intentions into something sordid. It's surprising, really, how easy it was. I can't believe it took me so long to figure out what to do.

That night I'd been petulant at dinner, just to stir you up.

'You're not eating much,' you pointed out.

'I never go *out*.' I was digging aimlessly at my food with the fork.

'I take you out.'

'With my *friends*, I mean.' I had no desire, of course, to waste my time with a bunch of teenagers. 'With people my *age*.'

'I know, I know.' You stopped eating, though your meal was only half-consumed, and laid your knife and fork across the plate. 'You shouldn't just spend your time with an old man.'

I flashed my most beautiful smile, to reward you for your deference. Then I ate a huge forkful of your special mashed potato. 'It's okay,' I said, speaking with my mouth full. 'I like your record collection. It's expensive to buy that stuff second-hand.'

You laughed ruefully. You were laughing at yourself, with me. I loved it when you did that. 'You like the eighties stuff, don't you?'

'Eighties? There's more seventies than eighties.'

You laughed again, but you didn't take up your fork.

I always teased you about your age when I felt bored, when I needed a reaction from you. It was such an easy thing. It was a perfectly natural thing for me to do. After all, I held all the aces—youth, beauty and cuteness. You were lucky I consented to live with you at all. But you were sensitive about it. The sense of urgency to make up for wasted time was everywhere about you. There was an edge to your indulgence of my jokes.

So I think maybe that's where the challenge in your eyes, later that night, came from.

We were lying together naked on the bed. I'd resigned myself to yet another dull, tender lovemaking session.

You slipped your hand between my thighs, as you always did.

'Mmmm,' I said, looking over your shoulder and counting the books on your bedside table.

I can remember when your fingers moved so gently I thought you were reluctant to touch me there, until I saw your eyes. They were always alight with hope. There was always a shy expectant smile on your face.

This wasn't like that at all. It wasn't that coaxing, hopeful tickling with which you'd first approached me. You were watching my face every second. But when I tried to meet your eyes, you'd flicker them away and watch the counterpane instead.

With a flash of inspiration, I changed tactics.

From that point on, when I was overcome with desire—or rather, when I wanted you to *think* I was overcome with desire—I pretended I was losing a battle. I acted as though you were making me get turned on. It seemed to you that I couldn't help myself, that I was relinquishing some control of myself to you. And, despite yourself, you found that hopelessly arousing.

I deceived you by such subtle means!

As you tried to arouse me, I made all the facial expressions that accompany blushes.

I winced, just slightly, at my wriggles of excitement.

As you kissed my nipples and made them hard, I lowered my eyes, flicking my gaze coyly into corners of the room, as the disconcerted do.

When you slipped fingers between my legs and found wetness, I rolled my eyes and pursed my lips and looked embarrassed.

Oh, darling, it made you mad! Mad for me, I mean, with that distressed, embarrassed lust I so much loved to see.

Thus, I made you master. Thus, I enslaved you.

When we actually fucked, you closed your eyes, unable to deal with the sight of what you thought you'd created. That was great. It gave my eyes free rein over your face, and I drank in every detail.

And the sounds! The sounds you made were exquisite to me. You breathed audibly, faster and faster, as though trying to drown out my own feigned whimpers of submission. And the smooth stream of your eloquence was churned and shattered by harsh rocks of words.

'I'm gonna—'

'I've gotta—'

'I'm fucken—'

Sometimes you'd loose even those last threads of sophistication, and descend wholly into guttural, staccato mumblings, devoid of all sense but a fierce animal appetite. You bayed and rumbled. These howls were broken with sharp splinters of obscenity.

'Fuck!'

Summer began. Everyone started coming to school in shorts. I noticed the tanned legs walking around me only in passing, and with derision. I felt myself to be magically pale, a nymph of the twilight. I wore my whiteness like a sorceress wears her robes. The stray light of the city came creeping even into our dark, curtained bedroom. I managed always to shimmer, to shine.

Under the electric light, I became hard and white and fluorescent. My palms and the soles of my feet were bright pink, like a mouse's paws.

But you softened that artificial light, lying on our bed with your bum in the air. You glowed yellow. Your skin was a pale olive colour. You made electric light seem like candlelight.

During the day, people started complaining about the heat. Mr Harrison saw me one sweltering day—I suppose it must have been a sweltering day—in stockings and a long-sleeved top. 'Bit warm for all that, isn't it?' he asked me, his lips pursed as if this were the punchline to a very clever joke.

I didn't reply. I hadn't even noticed the temperature.

It was hot but I felt cold. I was always cold, lately. My hands were always freezing. You used to clasp my fingers between your palms.

'Cold little hands,' you'd say, rubbing them, blowing on them. 'You need some sun.'

Sunshine had become strange to me. I was a creature who worked in small and intimate spaces. I liked to live in tents under blankets, in nests made of cushions, behind walls made of your limbs, under the roof of your chin. Whenever I went outside, I blinked in irritation.

I knew from what you'd written that you'd like to catch me masturbating.

I could tell from your notes what I was supposed to do, although it was an activity that was completely foreign to me.

So, one night, I arranged it.

I had already gone to bed. You were in the shower.

The bedroom was lit only by your bedlamp. Mine was out.

You'd decided that it was too hot for blankets, that night. They all lay where you'd folded them, on the chair by the bed. We had nothing but a pair of sheets to sleep between.

I waited until I heard the water stop running. Then I composed my limbs as if I were arranging flowers. I spread my legs—just slightly, not too far. I felt it was important to appear furtive rather than brazen. I covered my body with the sheet, right up to the neck. By twisting my head, I was able to observe the effect in the mirror. I was rather pleased with it.

The white sheet fell around me on every side, outlining all my limbs. The position of my hand was clearly observable. Perfect.

Silently, I waited for you. I didn't know what was going to happen, but my heart was beating fast with anticipation. I couldn't wait to see the look on your face.

You didn't disappoint me.

I had my eyes closed, when you came in. The scenario was only convincing if I seemed half-asleep, just absently touching myself. That's what you did, sometimes, in the mornings.

With my eyes still closed I couldn't see you, but I heard you stop dead in the doorway. The thought of your shock excited me and made my breath more shallow.

You cleared your throat, you darling! You were trying to give me a warning, a way out. I was annoyed. Your good manners, for the moment, had the upper hand over your lust.

This called for a more direct approach. I opened my eyes— lazily, as though I were just waking up. I stretched about a bit with my free hand, to add to this impression.

You were standing stock-still, your hair still wet and gleaming, wearing nothing but a hotel-stolen white towel.

'Hey, baby,' I said. I spoke just slightly too fast. This gave the impression that I was concentrating on my own private rapture.

'Hello.' You sounded miserably uncomfortable.

'It's okay,' I said, fixing my gaze solidly on your face. 'You can watch, if you like.'

And I kept moving my hand under the sheet.

I regarded you carefully. You took a few steps forwards, leaning slightly backwards, as though your head were more reluctant than the rest of your body. You licked your bottom lip, nervous as a lizard. It was an exciting sight.

'Your pupils are big,' you said. 'You look like a possum.'

I could have told just from the way your voice squeaked that you were aroused.

You stood there, in the middle of the room, bulging under your towel. I could hear you breathing.

'Honestly,' I said. I let you see me close my eyes, as though I wasn't particularly interested in you, and looked at you from between my eyelashes. 'I watch you, sometimes.' I yawned sensuously.

You jumped. 'When?'

'In the mornings. Before you're properly awake.'

That was a mistake. It gave you a way out. A way to equalise things. Eagerly, you said, 'Would you like to watch me? We could watch each other.'

'Fine,' I said, not showing my irritation at myself.

You let the towel fall to the floor. Selfconsciously, with a little reassuring smile at me, you took hold of your cock and started to move your hand up and down. You dug the other hand in underneath, pressing your testicles. The only thing you did which I liked was the little automatic gesture of licking your palm. That suggested long practice. I thought that you'd probably done that same quick movement every time you started to wank; ever since you were a boy.

I pulled myself up, so I was sitting with my back against the bedhead. I spread my legs further, more shamelessly, more (I presumed) sluttishly. I regarded you with what I hoped was a steamy challenge in my eyes. I was trying to manufacture sexual tension.

Tired of standing, you knelt down. You stumbled slightly, and had to put out one arm to steady yourself against the ground.

I giggled.

Looking up at me, you winced. You were slightly out of breath. 'You see?' With your arms, you indicated the whole room. 'That's what I—' You shook your head. 'You make me ... you get me down here, on my knees, cock in hand, looking like ...' You shrugged, shaking your head. 'And then you *laugh*.'

'I wasn't laughing,' I said, conciliatory. I folded my hands in my lap, demurely.

'Well, it's not a power-laugh, is it? You're not laughing to show me who's who. It's just *funny*.' Your hand tightened, as you looked at me.

I pouted, looking apprehensive—my panic safety-measure. 'Are you mad at me?'

You laughed dryly, shafting your hand up and down.

I regarded you with an uncomfortable, slightly fearful expression. It was the perfect mask. I was perving on your stress.

'I'm not *angry*!' You spat the word. There was appeal in your eyes. They were wet. This was suddenly much better. 'You're just ... you're like an animal. It's *chemical*, this.' Your eyes flickered downwards. 'You just *do* this to me. And I feel ... it's not even love, this.' You half-closed your eyes. Your arms shook as your hands speeded up. You spoke through your teeth. 'Just ... if you get lust, and you filter out all the checks and ... all the *shame* ... Just pure, physical, sensuous—' And you came, jerkily, all over the carpet.

Afterwards, I cried.

'It's not my *fault*!' I insisted tearfully. 'I don't *mean* to be like that.' I scrunched the tears from the corners of my eyes with the heels of my hands.

I was acting. I must have been. But something choked me, too, just slightly. Something felt faintly like real outrage; as though I really had been falsely accused.

You apologised, of course. It was pretty good. You kissed me all over, up and down my body, right down to my feet. You had tears in your eyes.

I played you like an instrument.

I spun it out for hours. I made the tears come rolling out down your cheeks. You knelt before me, your head bent in submission. You swore never, ever again to say anything to hurt me. You promised to take me shopping and buy me anything, anything at all that I wanted. There was a drawn, hunted look on your face as you said sorry and called me *Angel*.

I went to sleep in your arms, with you regarding my face anxiously, your eyes wide and worried. You clutched me so tightly that your hands sweated, and you smelled, most satisfyingly, of semen.

I may well have been dreaming. I couldn't tell, even at the time, if I was awake or asleep. But I thought you said something, long after I'd closed my eyes.

The voice was breathy, heavy with something. I couldn't tell whether it was tears or another, more violent passion.

I thought you said: 'I hate you, sometimes.'

I am afraid of my imagination. It's too powerful a force. It swamps me. It sweeps other people up and carries them away. There's a strange magic in me. If I think a thing hard enough, I can impose it upon the world.

It doesn't matter whether I want the thing to come true or

not. My imagination didn't care that you're a good man, that you meant well. It needed you to harm me. Effortlessly, it made you a monster.

The predatory creature I'd made of you began to hunt me.

Your eyes became narrow and luminous, like a cat's. I woke one night to go to the toilet and, coming back, I found you standing outside the door.

I was slightly startled. Never one to let an opportunity slip by, I pretended to be *very* startled.

'What are you …?' I asked blearily, wiping imaginary sleep from my eyes with my fists. The combination of the childlike gesture and my complete nakedness was a powerful one.

You looked guilty, covetous, hungry. 'I just wondered where you were,' you mumbled. Then you took my hand and led me back to bed.

On the couch, remember?

Hot and wilted from my walk home, I'd stretched myself out to sleep there. The light was purple and the air was heavy.

I woke to find your hand down my jeans.

'Hey!' I cried. In that first instant of awareness, I was genuinely shocked.

'It's okay. It's okay,' you said. 'I'm just.'

And you kissed me, hard.

Stroking my lips with one finger, you told me, 'They're so red.'

I wasn't wearing make-up. I never did. My blood just ran closer to the surface, these days.

I made no reply. I simply sat there trying to look cute and half-awake. I was glad I hadn't brushed my hair. The tousled, angelic effect was a good prop.

With your nose, you nuzzled between my legs.

It wasn't just a matter of giving me pleasure. It was dirtier than that.

You found little spurts of moisture and mumbled with triumph. The liquids of my body were prizes, now.

I'd made them so.

You thrust your hand beneath my nose. You watched to make sure I inhaled. The cloying smell stuck in my nose. It reeked of sweat and arousal. This was a new kind of violation. It was a kind of trophy, too: *Look what I caught! Look what I made you do!*

I lay flat, submissive. You swallowed the bait whole. Leaping onto the couch, a pirate onto a conquered ship, you pushed my legs apart as though they were inanimate, as though I was dead or unconscious.

You entered me without looking at my face. It was forceful and it hurt.

I dug into your back with my fingernails. No real passion spurred me on. It was a calculated action, like a bullfight attendant makes, tossing his darts scientifically into the back of the bull to enrage it at the right moment.

You gasped, wincing at your own guttural noise.

'Hey!' I said. I made you look at me, just briefly. I wasn't going to let you keep all those emotions, all that turmoil I'd worked so hard to create, to yourself. I needed to see them.

Your cheeks were dark purple, as though you'd been holding your breath.

Your eyes met mine with the full force of your challenge—lust, aggression, anger, all gathered together and thrust at me, like the point of a sword. But as I stared back, expressionless, they clouded with misery. Your pupils darted from side to side. They were schizophrenic eyes, which cannot trust the walls to retain their shape from one moment to another. You seemed every moment to fear a surprise attack.

I was hot on your trail now. The feelings of power, of lust, contracted my stomach. 'What do you want to do?' I asked sweetly, nearly choking on raw desire.

But you were beyond conversation. You panted loudly, and the sweat ran in little streams down your face. Your hair was all plastered down flat. Your eyes glazed over and you fixed your gaze on my shoulder.

All the tendons on your legs stood out. Your feet strained against the armrests. The whole couch shook and shuddered.

Staring at your incoherent animal eyes, I had a strange, prophetic feeling of apprehension.

I felt we were on a creaking boat, in the middle of a storm.

I felt we must capsize at any moment.

Over the next few days, I seemed to drift further away from the world with every moment. Suddenly there was only one tableau sucking me in.

I stopped talking almost entirely. In class, at school, I simply folded my arms and stared at the desk, waiting for it to be time to go home to you.

I found myself prey to strange nervousnesses brought about by still weather. I remember coming to absolute halts just standing at the side of the road, saturated with throttling, alien passions by a sudden lack of traffic noise.

Unexpected stillnesses—when the birds stop calling and you can't hear any traffic—filled me.

*

As I walked up the front path, I heard the telephone ringing. My hands trembled as I unlocked the door. They wanted me to *hurry, hurry, hurry.* I forced myself to be slow and calm.

Inside, I stood by the shrill screeching thing. I counted to ten. It stopped ringing. I thought I'd have a heart attack. But the telephone was just pausing to gather itself for another assault, like a baby breathing between screams.

A long time seemed to pass. I held myself still, sitting upright in the big armchair. That stillness was to make the time pass instantly, make it pass by without me, outside me. Deep within myself, I went into hibernation, waiting for you.

I heard your car turn into the driveway. I didn't move a muscle, but I was completely altered, as though I had been tuned into another frequency. You'd be watching me soon, infusing me with the strange energy of your awareness.

Outside, the car door slammed. Your keys clinked abruptly as you unlocked the door.

I waited in the wings. Only when you were in the hallway did I move. I timed everything perfectly. Just as you appeared in the doorway, I let you see me disappearing up the stairs.

'Hey!' you called.

I hardly saw the lines and angles of the stairs before me. I was choreographing the backs of my bare legs for you, willing them slimmer and more irresistible than ever.

I was beyond planning things. I was in the grip of the force that makes birds dance and stags fight and cats stalk about with their tails in the air.

I stripped quickly. I heard you mounting the stairs clumsily, unevenly, taking one, then two. Then one too heavily.

My clothes on the floor seemed too scrappy and diminished ever to have held me, like shed snakeskin. I rushed to take up the correct pose. Flinging the curtains back, I leant on the window ledge so that the slanting sunlight sheeted over me. The sun caught in the wisps of hair around my face and I saw glitterings like mica.

I stilled my whole body like a held breath, not wanting to waste an instant of consciousness that you wouldn't see.

Then with a whoosh you were there, you were present behind me, and I was properly alive again.

I felt you watching me. Your eyes slid all over my back, down my spine, down my legs.

You shuffled uncomfortably.

An intense heat swelled in my stomach and under my nipples. I was perfectly in control of my body, perfectly aware of how I must look from where you stood. White shoulder-blades, delicate hollows, little dancing ripples of light and shade. I stood still as a flower.

I overpowered you in an instant. You crossed the floor and pressed yourself into my back, gripping my arms below the shoulders. I didn't move or respond, but stood passive, half-limpid.

I felt your erection, defenceless against my back, through the scratchy surface of your trousers. I swelled inside, feeling it.

Your fingers dug into the soft skin on my arms. I hoped you wouldn't spoil things by speaking. I didn't want to be reduced from nymph to raconteur. You caught your breath and I knew you were trying to frame questions: Where've you been? Who were you with?

But at that moment, at the zenith of my powers, I could silence you with a thought. I made the tiniest, most delicate movement. I shifted position, rested my weight on the other leg. It was a disdainful movement. It meant: *Oh, so you're going to keep holding me, are you?*

This enchantment was impossible to resist. It brought you closer. It made you crush your chest into my back, link your hands around my chest, binding my arms to my sides. I could feel your anxiety in the unsmooth breath that blew over my neck, in the trembling of your knees and the white-knuckled tightness of your two hands.

I was the puppeteer and the puppet too. I slithered my hips from side to side, just gently, shifting my weight again. I turned my face further from you, tucking it into my chest. I let my hair fall between us like a curtain. Such a posture could have seemed frightened, vulnerable, but I infected it with slight, provocative boredom.

Your poor, powerless erection jumped and jolted. You made a little inarticulate noise of distress.

Every inch of my skin, every nerve of mine you touched, filled with blood and expanded. I saw your hands and they squeezed at me furiously, purple with the power of your grasp, but shaking from deep within, and with a desperate whiteness round the knuckles.

I couldn't titillate myself any longer. Turning, twisting round—but careful not to let you loosen your hold on me—I looked at your face. You were fierce, your brows all thundered together—but fierce like a boy who is frightened and embarrassed by his rage, a boy who cries when he is angry. You breathed between your teeth and seemed as usual to be trying to frame normal words, trying to think of some correct and proper sentence to set things right.

My heart beat faster. All my body seemed anaesthetised and swollen, fuzzily. You made some noise like 'Jhhh!' and seemed to be pleading, while you duelled. Your top buttons were undone. There was a little fluffy something in your hair. Oh, you were ridiculous, my angel.

I struggled against you. It was sensuous and calculated. You held my hands up above my head and I twisted from side to side, my face framed between the insides of my arms. I felt my wrists turning inside your hands. It was invigorating, like a massage. All my muscles warmed and tingled, as though I had been exercising.

You were shaking. You bared your teeth, resolute.

And now you bore down on me, turned me round, holding me by the wrists so that my toes just barely swept over the floor. I swooned as soon as I felt the bed behind my knees. I just *fell*, and took you with me, so that I lay below and you lay above, still holding my hands in that desperate vice.

I felt my lips pulsing as though swollen. I knew how red they must be. I let them part, and regarded you through my parted lips and my big eyes.

You couldn't help but kiss me. I lay as though in a faint and because I didn't respond you had to kiss me harder. Because I didn't part my lips wide for you, you had to force them open.

It was pure energy, to have you invade me like that. It was like entering the ocean or a storm, and lying limp in the grip of the elements.

Through my eyelashes I glimpsed wonders: the curve of your arm above my face, all muscles standing stiff, the skin glowing damp. You still held one of my wrists, up above my head.

I moved my free hand close to the captured one. I rubbed my wrists together.

You stilled completely. I heard the air pass between your lips with a rush.

You said with false, dangerous calm, 'Is that what you want?'

I lay mute beneath you, allowing your weight to squash the air out of my lungs.

Even then, you must have been willing me to say no, to scream, to end the game somehow. '*Is it?*' you demanded.

I said nothing.

'Right,' you said. You were brisk and adamant.

Then you moved and lay half-off the bed, though still with your fingers circled round my wrist, and I saw you fumbling on the floor among my clothes for stockings.

Then you sat astride my midriff, your knees pinning my arms. 'Right,' you murmured to yourself.

Each breath I took only seemed to skim the surface of my lungs. There passed across your face the most exquisitely transparent parade of emotions. I seemed to see them all distinctly, one after another.

Your nose seemed aquiline, your eyes haughty, your expression superior, businesslike. You twisted the stockings into ropes, pulling them sharply, testing. That efficiency, that interest in details, was alien, mesmerising.

Then I saw you with the mane of your hair all ruffled up behind your head, and your face seemed shadowed and bestial. I could see flecks of spittle glistening on your teeth as you tied the knots around my wrists, securing them above my head and then attaching them to the bedhead with a short lead. You were like a great ape bending over me.

As you bent your head to undo your zip, your cheeks seemed round and soft. You were lost again to childhood, to vulnerability, to the great concentration required of tasks performed for the very first time.

Then as you reared up, as you dug your arms under my stomach and rolled me over, you avoided my eyes, looking instead in that instant at my breasts, and there was that naked, crippling lust in your face, in the tip of your tongue between your teeth, in the loud breaths you allowed in between your teeth.

But in that moment, as your fingers beneath my stomach became ten hard points aimed at my soft belly, I became really afraid. As I rolled and the room around me rolled and disappeared, I caught my breath, feeling like a stone that's been turned over.

I didn't struggle. Like the condemned prisoner who accepts the proffered blindfold, spurning the last glimpse of sunlight on the leaves, I turned my face into the counterpane.

I could smell my hair on the pillow. The strawberry shampoo I'd chosen for its chemical, teenage scent seemed gritty, grainy, like strawberry pith.

My back was cold, now, without the counterpane against it.

Your hands all over my back were hot and damp. They seemed like cheap sensations; just pressures on my nerves; nothing more.

Sweat seemed to float on me like oil on a choppy ocean. I felt your teeth on the soft skin under my ear; and they were sharp and small and there seemed to be crocodile's rows of them, nipping away. I tried to shrug you off, but you just went lower, biting at my spine like a mosquito, impossible to swat.

Then I began to feel the real terror of confinement, white-blinded by the counterpane. I shifted uncomfortably, thinking perhaps I'd ask you to stop.

Your rough fingers under my legs drew them apart and I felt you sucking like some faceless thing—an oyster—at the ridge that divided my two holes.

'Yuck,' I whinged, with an angry little kick, like a child.

I expected you to respond to that. I expected you to ask if I was all right.

Then you were behind me, and I felt the knuckles of your curled fingers against my leg and I knew you were holding your cock and that's when I noticed that my wrists hurt. The stockings were too tight, I could sense a spreading blueness, a coldness, pins and needles, passing up the heel of my hand. I was pinned out like some amphibious creature about to be dissected.

Your fingers wormed around the edge of that hole, just tickling inside, and I was aware of a sudden urge to shit. Then you moved your hand away and I felt your fist around your cock against my arse and that's when I knew what you were going to do.

'No!' I said. 'Don't do that!'

I felt the tip, all hot and surrounded by sudden stinging fissures.

'I said don't do that!' I wanted to shout it but that way I was tied meant I couldn't find the breath. The words came out shallow and panted. You might not even have been able to hear me, with my mouth muffled against the sheets

I kicked wildly, or tried to. I wormed and squirmed my body from side to side.

I was really panicking now.

'Ow!' I was close to tears. You weren't listening. I couldn't turn my head. I wanted to look at your face, to see how to make you stop.

You didn't move or retreat. Instead you grabbed me round the waist so that I couldn't move to frustrate your efforts. Your fingers on my hips were hard and grasping.

You must have felt me trying to get away. You must have seen my hands twisting frantically, scrabbling at the bindings. You must have noticed me kicking as hard as I could. But you didn't stop.

Desperation overwhelmed me. Surely you wouldn't really do it? Not *now*? Not when I'd made it clear I didn't want you to?

I tried to scream. But there wasn't the air—

You were inside.

I thought you were going to break some membrane. I thought my intestines would rupture. I thought my insides must have sprung endless tiny leaks. I swear I felt all the fluids of my body trickling out and running down my legs.

I felt horrible. I stopped trying to struggle. It only made it hurt more.

You pushed and pushed and your breathing through clenched teeth seemed as much a pushing action as the movement of your hips, in and out like waves but moving ever closer like the tide was coming in.

I can't describe how powerless I felt, how stupid and crushed and defeated, like a mouse in a concrete mixer. I wished I could crawl out of my body and leave it on the bed for you.

You were grunting behind me. The noises were just disgusting; you sounded like a chimpanzee, and there was this horrible, inhuman slapping noise as your belly rhythmically slammed into my back.

It felt revolting. It was the most invasive act imaginable. Those parts of my body hadn't even existed until now. I hadn't needed them for my act. I had never looked at them; not through your eyes, or through my own.

I couldn't even control my breathing. Your weight kept winding me every time you came down on me, and I had to breathe in big ragged gasps, gulping for air like a goldfish.

You drove harder, but I hardly cared. I screamed thinly, with the back of my throat, like an ageing, see-through banshee. It was like giving up my soul.

I abandoned myself to the whirlpool.

The waters began to conify and spiral, as you pressed into me harder and grunted gutturally. I spun with them, choking on the spray.

Your arms reached out, covering my own, clasping me too tightly round the elbows, as you strained into me. I began to disintegrate in the water, to become long and thin and twisted. I swelled up and all my parts distended.

You pushed more desperately, bracing your feet against the end of the bed. My limbs and my head all came unstuck from each other, and spun round in the whirlpool separately, long liquefied streaks of me making circles in the water.

You reached the end, and, with a desperate little grunt, you came.

By this time I was only a stain in the water, churning round and round, all mixed up and dissolved.

You stopped.

I heard you talking, as though to yourself: 'Oh shit. Oh, *shit.*'

But I was nothing more than the white foam on the crests of little waves. I was gone.

*

What a consummate actress she was! Even torn in pieces, she remembered my lines.

Allowing my lower lip to tremble—a child betrayed—I said in the even tones of post-traumatic shock, 'I, um. Shit.' Shaking my head, bewildered. 'I just ... I didn't realise you were going to do that.' My thin wrists were braceleted with red marks where the cords had bitten. I rubbed at them, dazed, abstracted, eyes unfocussed on the wall.

You stood naked, stupid, flaccid, the stockings hanging limp in your hands. For you, the shock was real. Your knuckles, gripping my white bindings, were white.

I closed my eyes. I had to shut you out. I didn't want to see any part of you: not even your shadow against the wall. I screwed them up so tightly that I saw red explosions against the blackness.

I ran into the bathroom, where I could look at the cool white surfaces instead of at you. I let you hear me slam the door, click the lock.

Then all pretences dropped away and I was violently sick in the sink.

I hurt, I hurt, I hurt. This was far worse than losing my virginity. It burned like fire, and it was embarrassing, too: perverse. Humiliating.

The pain bent me double. I crouched down on my haunches, an injured beast.

Ugly drops of cum plopped onto the ice-white tiles. These globules were tinged pink, I realised with dull horror, with my blood. They had brown bits of shit in them. I wanted to be dead.

There was acid in my mouth, on my tongue. I was afraid.

I made animal keening noises in the back of my throat.

Crouched there, shivering, whimpering, under the towel rail, I was suddenly outside myself. I was a neighbour in a window, an actress on a movie screen, an anecdote overheard in a conversation between two strangers. My tears were bizarre, unnerving, *boring*: an unwelcome guest's unwelcome display of weakness. My situation seemed pathetic, my nakedness a needless melodrama.

There came a hammering on the door. 'Are you all right?' and a second later, loud with panic, 'Baby!'

My silence wasn't artifice.

My own intricate web of rules was ripped to shreds. I had bled as I had never allowed my imagined victims to bleed, cried as they'd never been permitted to cry, been caused pain which went beyond the sexual; or which was more mundane than the sexual.

I wanted to die.

Like any teenager, I had considered suicide before. A year or two earlier, one of my morbid fantasies had dealt with my slit wrists, my pale body floating in a blood-red, lukewarm bath. I was the Lady of Shalott, in a suburban bathroom. That imagined death had seemed fitting, grittily romantic. Now, your disposable razor by the sink, which awoke the possibility of a real end—here, soon—was not darkly poetic. It was plastic. It was bright yellow. It evoked nothing but an hysterical, chaotic passage from pain into oblivion. Death is a trauma, not a catharsis.

'Baby!' Your voice was high, frantic.

To staunch my fears I thrust my wrist into my mouth. I bit

down hard upon that round flesh.

In the mirror, I saw myself, all painted with the body's out-pourings.

I saw myself befouled.

Where I'd held my wrist against my face, there gleamed, visceral in the artificial light, a foul cascade of bodily waters—your ejaculate, my vomit, and my spittle.

I thought: Death always comes this way. It stalks us as a shadow, an idea. It floats above our lives, like an equation. Then it descends, and it is of the body. Blood and spit and spew belong to death. It is a dirty business.

Compare the ideal with the battle. Compare the cause with the fight. I saw noble pennants flutter in the wind. I saw corpses sprayed with blood, their faces muddied.

Like my subjugated creatures, I was beaten. But where my acts on them had been like logic, abstract, this act on me was concrete. It dribbled down my face and ran between my thighs—fluid, and certain.

This mess was the reality. It was punishment for my cleanly conceived thoughts.

'Baby?' you called, scratching on the door like an anxious pet.

I opened it, just a crack. But I didn't let you in.

I wasn't angry with you. I was like an octopus, instinctively squirting ink when provoked. Everything went black.

'Fuck off,' I said. I didn't even look at you. I blurred my eyes deliberately. 'Just leave me alone.'

You stood still for a few seconds. And then you moved away and disappeared and I heard the door slam downstairs.

Standing in the bathroom, bleeding, my arms empty, I began really to feel old.

T hank you for the money.

The first time I found one of those slim envelopes on the doormat and realised you'd been in the house, I thought it was a letter. I cried when I found the wad of fifty-dollar notes.

I haven't spent much of it, apart from the rent, of course. I'm keeping the rest for you, in a biscuit tin.

Then it was hard when I realised you were coming every Tuesday. I wanted to stay home from school when I knew you'd be coming, and look at you through the curtains. But I couldn't. The very thought reminded me of my horrible, destructive voyeurism, and I just couldn't.

Living alone and despairing like this, I have come to a terrifying awareness of the tragedy of the simple and the practical. Each morning, for example, I must wash my face. After dinner, I must brush my teeth. I do these things because I must—but each action has about it the worthlessness of finality, like the futile last meal a condemned prisoner eats before having his life snatched away. The basic, life-sustaining actions—the fork stabbing the potato, the chewing and the swallowing—are all about to be swept away before huge concerns, the soft embrace of the noose or the deadly current that runs through the chair; and yet, when the moment is appropriate, they must be performed, in full, stark awareness of their futility, the damnable smallness and forgettableness of them.

My actions—plaiting my hair, making a sandwich, pulling the covers over myself when I lay my body down in bed—are worse. Instead of the enormity of death they stand dwarfed before the enormity of human time. They are defiled by routine. Tomorrow and tomorrow and tomorrow are bad enough. The thought of the insufferable future freezes my mind, makes me close my eyes with an insidious, *still* terror. But *today*! Today, and today, and today, this eternity the present, make my heart beat fast with disgust and with fear.

I feel as though my brain is running to fat, or is puffy and misted with tears, like my eyes.

The house looks pretty bad. I can't be bothered doing the washing up. I leave the plates where they stand, with the forks still in them.

You aren't here to finish the painting. I haven't done any more. I don't know how. The wall in the hall outside our bedroom is half tobacco-stained off-white and half pastel-cream. There's a wavering line between the old coat and the new. It looks pitiful, like the hurriedly abandoned homes of evacuees.

I find myself flicking through your scribbled notes. It's not that

I want to read the subject matter. I just like looking at your handwriting.

I don't know if I quite believe all this stuff I've read about handwriting experts, who claim that the formations of letters on the page represent a kind of emotional contour map. Yet I've spent so much of the afternoon looking at these curly lines, that the bright sun has all leaked away and I've had to turn the light on.

Your lower-case n's are straight on the left and dip down sharply on the right. They remind me of the movement of your hips when we made love, that carnal spasm of your lower body which sometimes so embarrassed you in your dignity and sophistication. 'Any dog can do this,' you said once in disgust. Poor angel.

Your o's are bigger than they need to be; sensuously over-sized. They make me think of a time when we sat topless, kissing, on this exact couch. I fiddled with your belt and you pushed my hand away, saying, 'No...no, just let me touch you,' moving your hands in sweeping gentle circles over my skin.

I know I must seem humourless. I can't remember the last time I found anything funny. I suppose it's because, for a thing to seem funny, it must disturb the order of things. That's why movie audiences laugh at businessmen falling over. But everything whirls so impossibly around for me. I haven't any set of standards to judge funniness against. Nothing seems ridiculous. Everything's uncertain.

Often I'm just sort of *knowing*—in the same way that the sky is just sort of *up there*—that of course I am just a creature that suffers and suffers.

But, at times, I find myself spreading butter on my toast. I find myself lying on my back in the bath, hair spread out in the water, shaking out the shampoo with my fingers. And these little actions are utterly painless.

I wonder what I'd say to you. If I heard your key in the lock, at this moment. If I heard you jogging on your toes up the stairs to this room. If you sauntered in and, sitting on the edge of the bed, smiled and said, 'All is forgiven.'

Speaking to you, I would be spitting out the splinters of teeth and the mess of blood that are all that remains of my chewed-up mind. I wouldn't plead unmitigable sorrow, endless suffering. I wouldn't display my despair proudly, as an acknowledgement of guilt and proof of redemption.

I'd say: 'Tell me something.' I'd say: 'I don't know what to *think*.'

Mr Harrison knows; or he guesses. I've shown him, somehow. According to some deeper will, I've acted moments of stress, of abandonment. I've closed my eyes in pain when it looked as though I thought no-one was looking. I knew his eyes were on me.

I've awakened his curiosity, almost deliberately. When I walk past him, all my powers coalesce and he can't help but watch me.

He asked me to stay back after class yesterday. Everyone glanced at me, casually curious, as they scooped up books and papers and left.

I sat. I was frozen. I thought about momentary lapses of

concentration, spinning wheels, twisted metal. It seemed incongruous.

Palms down on the desk in front of me, he balanced on straight arms, and raised one eyebrow.

He was closer to me than he'd ever been before. That unfamiliar smell, a cocktail of medicines and cheap shampoo, wafted over me. I didn't move. The strangeness of him cut into me.

'Is everything all right?'

I couldn't tell him the truth. I didn't have time to formulate a lie. 'Yeah.' I leaned backwards slightly. I had to get away from that smell.

He misjudged my action and stepped back, embarrassed. I realised, a second too late, that he thought I was telling him he was too close for comfort.

'Sure?' He half-shrugged, arms extended, in apology.

I said nothing. The hairs on his arm were all swept against the grain. I wanted vaguely to brush them back the right way.

His upturned palm seemed to be waiting for something to land on it from above.

He took a breath, preparing to speak. Then his hand closed on empty air, and he turned away.

It was an anticlimax.

I was almost disappointed.

I fantasise about absolution.

I close my eyes, and give myself cancer. I lie in a hospital bed, a living skeleton, skin stretched tight over riddling malignancies.

There are two versions of this fantasy.

In the first, which I have usually in the mornings, you never come to see me. I lie there, waiting and waiting, thinning and thinning, coughing and coughing, but you don't come.

The Catholic priest drops by. He's fat and well meaning. He leaves prayer cards and pamphlets in a pile by my bed. I get sicker as the pile gets higher. One day, the priest asks me if I would like him to give me confession. I say that you are the only person I would possibly want to confess anything to. Half-forgotten snippets of church monologues float through my mind: '... in my thoughts and in my deeds ... in what I have done and in what I have failed to do ...' Sixteen years old and hopelessly alone, I stare at the ceiling, waiting to slide into that unknowable blackness. It seems only fair.

In the second version, which tends to hit me late at night, when midnight melodrama seizes my tired mind, you come rushing in at almost the last moment. You take my limp, clammy fingers and press them to your lips. You're crying. I tell you not to. I say, 'It's only fair.'

I'm getting a bit self-indulgent now.

I've told you my story. I've communicated my apologies. I've found an envelope and written your name on the front. I'm just delaying the moment when I'll have to seal all this away and give it to you.

I don't want to. I think about how much safer and more satisfying it would be to let you go on bearing the great weight of guilt for what has happened. I know that guilt. I know it's mine. But it crushes me, do you understand? It presses me down and empties me all out. I wish there was some way I could let you keep it, just keep it away from me. But I can't.

Not without it destroying you, and I can't let that happen.

I will have destroyed myself, with this letter. Or at least, I will have destroyed the image of myself I'd created in your mind. It's hard to let it go. It's all I have.

P ostscript

I *knew* you were going to hate me for this.

I *knew* you'd be furious. I *knew* you'd feel foolish and deceived.

Tuesday has come again, and this morning I left it on the front mat where you'd be sure to see it when you came to give me the money. I could hardly bear to put it down. My hand sweated, gripping it, and the ink in your name started to run.

When I came home from school and saw it was gone, I felt sick. Really darkly nauseous, as though I had food poisoning.

I was nervous, too. It was like being a child again. I knew I'd been bad and I knew I was going to get in trouble and I just had to sit there, swallowing my fear, and wait.

I couldn't speak when you came inside. I just stood at the bottom of the stairs, holding the polished banister-head.

'How've you been?'

Your question seemed forced, formal; a matter of protocol. Knowing in my heart that I'd lost you, I threw caution to the wind, and spoke with unguarded honesty.

'Terrible,' I told you, my eyes on yours, my eyelids drawn like open curtains, so that, for once, you could truly see right into the room beyond. 'Miserable. I've been crying and crying.'

Framed in the doorway, you remained silent. Your head moved imperceptibly from side to side. This might have been an expression of disgust for my non-existent innocence; but then again, it may merely have reflected your own perplexity.

'What about you?'

That familiar laugh through the nose, at the superfluity of the question. 'About the same,' you said. 'Pretty miserable.'

Everything hung silent around us for a moment. Then you broke through the static air, moving towards me. Closer you came and closer. I couldn't move.

You put your arms around me.

I thought I'd disintegrate. I thought I'd open up, that every cut or scratch I'd ever suffered would unheal itself and flow again. I thought I'd bleed all away before your eyes, and soak into the carpet.

All my nerves were dead. I couldn't feel a thing, except a vague animal trembling deep within. Leaning back, you put your hands on my shoulders.

'It's okay,' you said, like the Risen Christ.

I found a tongue to speak, and the words came old and withered, dry and ancient, as clipped as the Sibyl's. 'No,' I said. 'Don't be stupid!'

As you used to do, you smoothed back strands of hair behind my ear, smiling gently all the while.

It was infuriating, intolerable.

'Didn't you read my letter?'

'Course I did.'

'It's all true,' I told you bluntly.

'I know.'

I stood before you, five foot two inches of stiff and bristling pride. I wanted to shout: 'You *see* what I am? You *see* this? This creeping beast, which I with words and voice and gestures have contained?' I bit down with my molars on the inside of my mouth. I thought I might cry from frustration.

'You must hate me,' I said.

Your mouth twisted awkwardly, with that familiar easy pity. Gently, you asked, 'Why should I hate you?'

Now that my secret was out, I spoke without pseudo-emotion: one adult to another. 'I'm a pervert,' I said, shrugging my shoulders.

'No, you aren't!' you told me severely. 'You're just a ... a little *girl*!'

'But I—' I tried to insist.

Schoolmasterly, you asserted, 'Perverts are people who *act* on their perversions.'

'I did!' I protested. There was some blockage in my throat which choked my voice. You kept on as though you hadn't heard.

'They're everywhere,' you told me earnestly. 'There are brothels and bookshops full of them. They're all over the Internet, swapping pictures and e-mailing each other filthy messages. They steal children from parks. They leave their menace hanging around us like ...' You struggled for a metaphor. '*Smoke!* My sister had to check for madmen under the bed and killers behind the curtain *every night* before she could sleep! For all I know, she still does it. Oh, Angel ...' You shook your head. You swallowed. You rubbed your mouth with one hand. There were, I noticed with a shock of exquisite guilt, tears in your eyes.

Surely, surely, you couldn't be so badly mistaken as still to love me?

I wanted to ask, You don't still love me, do you? But I didn't.

My hand fluttered against your thigh. I winced against my familiar inability to make fine or gentle movements without trembling. 'I'm shaking,' I said. 'I *always* shake.'

Pulling away, drawing back, looking at me squarely, you said, 'Can't you understand? I love you *because* you shake.'

'I can't say, *I love you!*' I whined, in my petulant-little-girl voice. There were tears in my eyes. Real ones. 'I can't even *smile*...' I grimaced appealingly, through my tears. It was hopeless.

I pressed a finger to the corner of your eye, and then drew a snail-trail of tears down your cheek.

'They look real,' you told me.

'I know,' I said. 'But so do the fake ones!'

I needed you to understand. I widened my eyes in sincerity.

Hysteria welled in my gut. All the treasures of the world twinkled before me, in your green irises, and I was powerless to grasp them. I would have to watch as the world's substance and mine ripped them from my sight.

'Even this—' I pointed at my distraught face—'it's fake!'

'It doesn't matter,' you said, running a finger down my cheek, just as you used to. 'I'll believe you.'

My heart sank for my wickedness. 'I'm terrible,' I said.

'You're a very good person.' You sweated with the effort of trying to make me understand. 'You've just been given a terrible *shape*. You've been very good, inside it.'

You looked straight at me, and in your face there was no trace of disgust, but only the most profound and loving pity.

You said, 'You were only doing what comes naturally.'

And then something made itself clear to me. I learnt a truth.

It was a truth more harsh and holy than any that are simply to do with the way things are. It was higher and more profound than any of those interpersonal recipes I've discovered.

I understood that there is another path to innocence; that it can be attained, like wisdom. I knew that I am a kind of Holy Innocent, after all. One of God's special cases. Blundering around inside my own instincts, handicapped.

I'm like a Holy Idiot; a retarded child who is closer to Heaven because of his disability. A kind of holy pervert, who struggles every day to be good.

'I just want ...' you said. 'I just want to put all that away. All those dark things. I just want—'

You kissed me on the cheek, with your lips closed. It was infinitely soft and chaste. I nearly fainted.

'You're such a *baby*!' you whispered.

You're still my darling. You're just the same.

You're living as though faith has been restored to you.

You're so careful of me. You iron the sheets before you make the bed. You spend hours cooking. You make me swallow vitamin pills and drink extra milk.

You've been working on the house. You finished the walls upstairs. Now everything in the study is wrapped in splattered white sheets. You whistle endlessly while you paint. You whistle tunes from beginning to end, perfectly, without missing a note.

You laugh so intensely, when you catch my eye. You're sharing an understanding with me. I smile back, so you'll know

I've understood.

I've found the perfect expression for those moments. It's like emergency joy. I smile suddenly, forcefully. It's as if I'm so happy that I've been left with no option but a huge, wordless grin.

You talk to me about your plans: to finish renovating the house; for the two of us to go overseas at the end of the year. I nod, lips parted, and seem enthusiastic. My eyes never glaze. I'm too careful for that. But when I'm sitting on your lap, and you're doing nothing but talk, sometimes I can't control the thoughts that come to me. They just slide into my mind.

More and more often, I find myself thinking about Mr Harrison.

Almost accidentally, I've wondered what he would think if he were made to understand about you and me. He could perhaps be shown the love bites on my neck when I raise my hand to ask a question. I could perhaps act caught out, and cover them with one hand, bristling with pride.

I could seem pitiable, manipulated, virtuous. I could seem as though I'd been taken advantage of, confused, made old. I could defend you, with tears in my eyes. He might touch my shoulder and say, 'This should never have happened to you.'

One day, he might find himself so overwhelmed with pity that he kisses me.

I'm repairing the fort, shoring up the moat, massing the men, drilling the army, building tunnels deep below the earth. If I am stormed, routed, I shall at least have a retreat.